THE URBANA FREE LIBRARY

3 1230 00966 9983

S0-CFJ-949

PRAISE

A beautifully written novel about love and disappointments, about the bonds we make and the ways they strengthen or break in moments of crisis. Filled with personality, earthy, guttural, the prose of the novel is crisp and suffused with poetic sentences. The setting details are vivid—the juniper trees, the caves, the mud brick stove. The landscape comes beautifully alive, as do other plot points in *During-the-Event's* journey.

> —Chinelo Okparanta, 2018 Permafrost Prize Judge and author of *Under the Udala Trees* and *Happiness, Like Water*

Roger Wall's splendid, hauntingly strange *During-the-Event* strikes deep emotional chords. Part dystopian tale, part timeless allegory, part eulogy for the memorable Ancient Mariner figure of Otis, this is a beautifully cadenced novel with a philosophically melancholy heart.

> —Howard Norman, author of *The Ghost Clause*

Set in a brutal time, when the havoc of global warming and rising seas have resulted in mass extermination and machine rule, Roger Wall's *During-the-Event* brings a vivid warning. Through the innocent eyes of one young survivor, however, we experience the intricate delicacy, still, of creation, and a persistent journey toward renewal.

> —Diane Simmons, author of *The Courtship of Eva Eldridge*

The Urbana Free Library

To renew: call **217-367-4057**
or go to **urbanafreelibrary.org**
and select **My Account**

DISCARDED BY THE
URBANA FREE LIBRARY

DURING-THE-EVENT

DURING-THE-EVENT

A NOVEL

University of Alaska Press
Fairbanks, Alaska

Text © 2019 Roger Wall

Published by
University of Alaska Press
P.O. Box 756240
Fairbanks, AK 99775-6240

Cover design by Martyn Schmoll.
Interior design and layout by 590 Design.

Author photo by David Current.

Library of Congress Cataloging in Publication Data
Names: Wall, Roger, 1955-author.
Title: During-the-Event : a novel / by Roger Wall.
Description: Fairbanks, AK : University of Alaska Press, [2019] |
Identifiers: LCCN 2018029047 (print) | LCCN 2018030477 (ebook) | ISBN
    9781602233836 (ebook) | ISBN 9781602233829 (pbk. : alk. paper)
Subjects: | GSAFD: Dystopian fiction.
Classification: LCC PS3623.A4428 (ebook) | LCC PS3623.A4428 D87 2019 (print)
    | DDC 813/.6dc23
LC record available at https://lccn.loc.gov/2018029047

To Jan & Barret

PART I:
OTIS

"I want to see my grave. To make sure you've dug it properly."

Otis spoke those words the day before he died. We were in the cave in Windy Butte, our home in the White Earth River valley in the former state of North Dakota. Otis was at the back of the cave, where the air was cool and damp, in a bed he'd made by nailing together peeling clapboard that he'd scavenged from the ruins of the Catholic church. I was standing near the cave's entrance, beside the mud brick stove he'd built when I was an infant. (He'd worked with me strapped to his back with a strip of blanket, he'd told me.) I was holding a pot of corn mush and looking across the valley to Cemetery Butte, where I should have been digging his grave.

He said the first part, "I want to see my grave," in a quiet, weak voice—maybe he had just woken up—but the words made me stop chewing and hold off on taking another spoonful of mush. I peered into the dim light at the back of the cave where he was rustling around.

He had thrown off the rabbit-skin blanket and was struggling to sit up. The bed squeaked. He coughed and hawked up phlegm, cleared his throat. Then in a stern voice, he said the second part, "To make sure you've dug it properly."

1

He seemed to accent "properly," as though he knew what I had been up to that morning: not digging his grave on Cemetery Butte but sailing the canoe on Lake Sakakawea, an act that put me at risk of drowning and us at risk of detection, or so Otis would have reasoned. He seemed to fear being rounded up by government agents more than he feared death, although neither he nor I, alone or together, ever encountered an agent in all of our days in White Earth River, perhaps because Otis sometimes rushed me into the basement or up to the cave to avoid what he insisted were agents slinking into our town.

I didn't answer Otis right away, since I hadn't expected that he'd want to inspect the grave and was worried he'd notice that I hadn't dug it to his specifications. His breathing had become heavy in the past few days, as though he had to push each breath through a handful of silt to get it out. But I figured he could survive a trip up the butte. He was a tough old coot.

"Once I finish eating, I'll take you there. On my back," I said and then sunk the spoon into the pot of corn mush. I was starving.

"I don't know about that," Otis said.

"Do you want some of this?" I asked.

I held up the dented pot toward Otis. He was resting against the juniper trunks that lined the cave wall. He shook his head. There was hardly any mush left, anyway.

"Why are you stooped over?" Otis asked.

"My back is tired."

"You look guilty."

Otis seemed to know whenever I disobeyed one of his rules.

"It's a weak posture, you'll injure yourself in the garden," he said. "Try to avoid it, for your own sake." He hawked some more phlegm.

"Okay."

I scraped the last scoopful from the pot and then dunked it into the wash pail.

"I'll need my sweater. The cool season has come early this year," he said.

"The warm season has just begun," I corrected him. "You've been in the cave too long. You need some sun, that's all."

Where the light from the cave entrance fell off, a dresser stood with half of a broken mirror propped against the wall. I yanked on the mismatched knobs to open the warped top drawer. Inside, Otis's red wool socks and navy blue sweater were arranged right to left.

The air at the back of the cave smelled of Otis, not just the usual smell of his body but also of his urine and feces. He hadn't washed in a few days. Neither had he cleaned his teeth with the stick, which was perhaps why his breath smelled sour. Or maybe his lungs were infected and he was exhaling bits of decay and pus when he coughed up phlegm. I knelt on the willow matting and began to dress him.

"Okay, give me a foot," I said and rolled the red socks over the white cotton ones he had darned so many times that the toes and heels were a crosshatch of black threads. Over the socks I tied the wide deer-hide straps of his rubber sandals. I wore a pair of these, too; we had made them from the garden cart's flat tire.

"Up with the arms," I said.

I slid the heavy navy blue sweater over his head and then brushed wisps of thin gray hair out of his face and tucked them into his braid.

"There. Climb on up, now. Come on. Wrap your arms around my chest."

I squatted, with my back toward him, and grabbed his bony thighs, one in each hand. He fell against me, and I hoisted him up into the small of my back.

"Don't drop me down the butte," he said.

He sounded scared, so I tried to make a joke: "You think you'll be so lucky? Just hold on tight."

Otis gripped my arms, but as I stepped forward, he swayed backward and groaned in panic. I countered by jerking him into my back.

"I told you to hold on!" I shouted.

"I'm so weak," he whispered in a hoarse voice.

"Okay, let me get my footing, here," I said.

The willow mats covering the cave floor flexed under our weight. I couldn't see very well in the shadows. Otis had skinned the bark off the junipers to brighten the walls, but the split beams that held back the crumbly sandstone ceiling were covered with a film of soot and grease from cooking and seemed to swallow light. I crouched so Otis wouldn't bump his head or smudge the figures I had drawn in the grime when I was young.

"Sunshine! I bet that feels good!" I said, trying to sound cheerful, when we reached the cave's entrance. Otis's skin had turned yellow over the past few days, and I hoped the sun would make it bronze again.

"I've never seen such bright light," Otis said.

"It's always like this."

Maybe his vision was off; the whites of his eyes had become as yellow as his skin.

I cinched him up onto my hips and started down the wind-scoured trail, avoiding the steep sandstone flanks that I usually took to and from our cave in Windy Butte. Its flanks were so dry that they seemed incapable of supporting life, but as I carried Otis through a maze of low outcrops, we passed clumps of rabbit bush, goldenrod, and grasses, which were enough to interest the pronghorns whose faint tracks I often followed along this south-facing slope. I never saw them, only their hoof prints. Sometimes I thought the prints were from animals in the spirit world that Otis spoke of; perhaps their spirits lived in the cracks and crevasses and hollows of the butte so they could see their still-living brothers and sisters walking the trails and grazing in the terraces below. I was afraid of disturbing them.

"And you thought I'd drop you, huh?" I joked when we reached the base of Windy Butte. I was relieved I hadn't and thought I deserved a little praise, which Otis provided by saying, "This is nice, being carried. You've become a strong boy. We'll have to do this again."

His breathing was calm, now; it didn't sound gravelly.

"Sure, we'll do it tomorrow. We can do it everyday."

I lingered, there on the terrace, with Otis pressing into my back, and thought how well he'd done. He was fine. He wasn't going to die anytime soon, I thought. I'm sure I was smiling, but Otis couldn't see my face, and he didn't say anything else.

From the base of Windy Butte, a series of terraces ran stepwise down to the road and garden along the White Earth River. During that period of my life, when Otis was dying and I was making daily trips from the cave to the garden and then Cemetery Butte and sometimes the boathouse, the terraces represented an in-between ground. Their lower elevation spared them from the dry wind higher up on the buttes, but they were well enough above the bottomland not to be haunted by the ghosts of the town people who used to tend the gardens along the river. Nor were they desolate like the abandoned boathouse and playing field and the jagged and flattened ruins of the town. They were gentle, rolling, and undisturbed, the only place in the valley not scarred by destruction or loss, and seemed to be waiting for a person to settle on their slopes and make a fresh start: the hillocks of grass, the gray leaves of sagebrush and willow, delicate ephemerals, and the spikes of orange and the soft purple of Indian paintbrush and coneflowers on the gentle slopes; and groves of box elder, a solitary elm, a patch of June berries, and a stand of choke-cherry signaling that somewhere among the trees and shrubs there was enough moisture to provide a reliable trickle for drinking water. We should have lived there, instead of in the cave, especially once we were sure no one was going to wander into our valley.

I avoided the ruins of the town, which were far down and off to the right. Otis went limp as I crossed the road. For a moment I thought he had fallen asleep. I stopped short on the path to the garden and tightened my grip on his thighs. I shouted his name and bounced him up and down. He started to wheeze and then gasped.

"You're hurting me," he moaned.

I turned my head and spoke over my shoulder: "I didn't want you to miss anything."

"I'm not."

"Okay, then."

I backed him onto the bench in the cottonwood grove on the edge of the garden. A light breeze made the leaves tremble and show their pale undersides. Their sound calmed me. It was like the sail vibrating in the wind or water rushing along the hull of the canoe, but the sound of the leaves didn't make me afraid, as the sound of the sail or water did. Otis's wheezing became louder. His thin, bony frame rose and fell.

"I should've brought a blanket for you to sit on," I said. "The bench . . ."

"I've sat on harder things," he cut me off. "Ever wrap your legs around a steel girder? Now that's hard. And cold! Up in that god-damn wind? Makes your balls run for cover."

I started to laugh. Otis's stories about iron work in the Center were some of my favorites, except for the one about the man who slipped off a beam and fell ten stories and died.

"I used to kiss Malèna on this bench," Otis said. "After everyone else had finished working in the garden for the day and had gone home. I liked to kiss her to the sound of the river."

He rubbed the smooth, worn bench with his fingers and looked away, avoiding my stare. I didn't say anything.

He swallowed once and then looked me in the eye: "But I didn't kiss her on the cheek, like I kiss you," he said.

I worried that the story of kissing Malèna would remind him of her death, how her fever had forced Otis, perhaps, to stop kissing her and, before he knew it, take her on the train to the Center, where she died in a hospital, his last kiss probably on her forehead. She died before I was born.

"You want some water?" I almost shouted at him.

"I'm not drinking anymore."

"Oh, yes, you are. Of course, you are."

I dropped a grimy white plastic bucket knotted to a stiff gray cord down the defunct town well and listened for the splash, and then pulled until a half-bucket of foul, mineral-laced water appeared. I waited for the sediment to settle before pouring Otis a tin cup of the salty liquid. When I returned to the grove of cottonwoods, he was slouched forward with his hands folded in his lap. He reached for the cup and then gulped down the water. It seemed to give him energy because he cleared his throat, straightened his back, and said in a strong, energetic voice:

"Tony LePerle was a moron. He was a moron before and a moron afterwards."

I was relieved that Otis was telling *our* story, the one about the destruction of the town and our survival, "The Vision Foretelling the Event and the Escape to Destiny," and seemed to have forgotten his memories of kissing Malèna on the bench.

Otis had created our story around the time I was learning to read. It was more compelling than any of the simple ones I could struggle to read out loud, and every night I begged to hear it. With each retelling Otis added more detail and dramatic pauses and experimented with when to smile, frown, and meet my eyes to draw me into the action. The story's pull, like a strong current, was too great to resist. Sometimes I resented becoming caught up in it, but that day, with Otis sitting on the bench, I was eager to play my part: our story gave him life. Although Otis could enter the story anywhere, his favorite place was the murder that Tony LePerle had committed.

I nodded my head in agreement and fed Otis the line that he needed to work up a fine rage, which would keep me on the verge of laughter for most of the story:

"Yes, he shouldn't have returned," I said.

I had to say this with anger, a touch of hatred. If I really wanted Otis to hoot and holler, I'd add, "that dirty half-breed son of a bitch." That day, under the cottonwoods, I didn't include the epithet, so he wouldn't exhaust himself too quickly.

"I'm glad he got the job, because his family needed the money," Otis continued. "But he was a moron. He wasn't one of us. His father was a white, from up north, what used to be Canada. Good-for-nothing blood. His mother made a mistake. But we couldn't turn her son away."

"That's right. What else could you do?" How many times had I said this? "What else could you do?" I loved saying that line.

Tony LePerle was in the Water Corps, stationed in what was at the time Rugby, North Dakota, which is now the Center, the capital of the North American continent. When Tony was sent to Bismarck with a crew to cut that city off from the water grid, a group of old people confronted him, told him that without water they'd die. He shut off the valve anyway, and they probably did die, but his guilt made him run home to White Earth River. He boasted that he'd expose what the government was really doing: outright slaughter of people it couldn't use, didn't want to relocate, and couldn't feed. But Sammy Goldrausch, the government representative in White Earth River, silenced the computer network that connected the town to the rest of the continent before Tony could send out his first message. Then, when Sammy tried to arrest him, Tony got his shotgun from his mother's house and pumped a .12 gauge deer slug into Sammy's chest. A town council discussion about whether or not to escort Tony to the Center and give him up dragged on for several nights. Factions developed, arguments broke out, and the few young men living in the town appeared at meetings armed with hunting rifles.

"Sammy wasn't typical government," Otis continued. "He'd read books about the Hidatsa, danced at powwows, gambled at the old casino. He was my friend. Killing him was wrong. We should've surrendered Tony. But he had that gun, as did the other young men. They got riled-up, thought they could protect themselves, defend the town. Everyone became afraid, of him, of his friends, of the government. If it weren't for Tony LePerle, we could've lived out our lives in peace."

"Yes, then they sent Helicopter."

I used my most serious voice to say this because it would let Otis pause and rest his fury. He was already breathing hard. We were, too, entering a more desperate part of the story, where not just one person was murdered but the whole town was destroyed.

Otis's convention of personifying the machinery that carried out the destruction may sound childish (I was a child when I adopted this practice), but to Otis, and to me as well, the machines the government used against us had the aura of flesh-and-blood giants.

The government had targeted the windmills that powered the town and sent a helicopter to drop something, a cable, perhaps, to disable and break the turbines, disrupt the town's energy supply. This all occurred before I was born, but I've climbed to the top of Windy Butte a few times—again breaking one of Otis's rules—and found a few of the old wind turbines still standing on the prairie, their blades idle, squeaking in the breeze.

"I could hear the towers crashing to the ground! A whining, steel colliding into steel!" Otis's voice rose. "Government thought that without electricity we'd give up Tony LePerle. No sewer, no water, no heat. It was the cool season, remember. A few people left on bicycles, but the rest of us hung on. Resolute. Tony LePerle used his ammunition to kill deer, once a stray cow. We ate very well."

Otis looked content, wheezing on the bench, as though he had just killed the cow himself and could remember how the meat had tasted, whether it was oily, well salted, perhaps rubbed down with black pepper, a spice he sometimes spoke of but which we never found in the destroyed kitchens in the town's ruins.

"But you knew they would send Machine," I said to keep the story moving.

"Yes, Machine came," he stated and then stopped and opened and closed his eyes and rubbed his thumbs together over folded hands, as though he was trying to remember what happened next. "Come on, man, you know how it goes!" I should have said. Or, "Take a breath!" But I didn't; instead, I blurted out:

"Just like in your vision, right?"

I realized my mistake immediately. I gripped the handle of the knife hanging from my belt. I wanted to cut myself to draw his attention away from that word. *Vision.*

Otis swept the tin cup off the bench. It rolled in the dust. Water spilled on the dusty ground.

"Take me to my grave!" he shouted, and then started wheezing hard, his chest pumping in and out under his shirt.

"Yeah, we'll do that right now," I said. I went over to the bench and backed into him, grabbed his arms, and snapped him onto my back. He gasped, as if I were about to throw him over my head.

When I was probably fourteen or fifteen, I had started to notice that Otis couldn't work as long and hard as he used to. I began to think about my parents, Javier and Maria. Our life would be easier, I had pointed out to Otis while we were weeding, if they were here to help us. Then I'd asked, "Didn't your vision show you what happened to them?"

Otis had answered in a flat, weary tone, speaking more to the ground than to me: "Our life—this is all the vision showed me."

His response had angered me, and I had wanted to hurt him. I had straightened up on my knees and said, "I guess they wouldn't have wanted to live with you, anyway."

Otis had glared at me and shouted: "Give up, is that what you want? Wander across the prairie looking for them? End up at an agricultural preserve? A strip mine? The Center? Agents would detect us before we knew it. I'm still in the database. An old man like me they'd shoot right on the spot and splay for the vultures to eat. And they'd probably kill you, too, just to save time. Two shots. Bang, bang. They wouldn't even stop their truck. This land is what we were

11

given. Our purpose is to work it and defend it with our lives. Your parents are dead!"

I had walked away at that point and sat in the river. Otis had never before said they were dead; just that he didn't know what happened to them. We only found skeletons in the demolished houses, none on the playing field where town people had gathered to roast animals during the period before the town was destroyed.

A few days later I had asked Otis if we could perform a burial ceremony for my parents, bury two remnants of wallboard on Cemetery Butte, but Otis had resisted: "We don't want building materials to pollute the earth up there."

For a while after that I had carried two pieces of concrete in my pocket, but they had worn a hole in my shorts and had fallen out.

The next time Otis had told the story, he hadn't shouted, "They were murdering us!" and raised his hands above his head as though he were receiving the glorious vision that had showed us the route through lingering clouds of dust to destiny, a new life as traditional Hidatsa Indians, with me riding on his shoulders to scout the way up the terraces to the cave. Instead, he had focused on the stupidity of Tony LePerle, or the sadness of Sammy Goldrausch's murder, the brutality of the government's response, things we could get worked up over. He never used the word *vision* again.

I pulled him tight against my back to calm his angry breathing. As we humped across the footbridge over the White Earth River, he wrapped his arms firmly around my stomach and panted over my shoulder. I'm sure his foul breath made me frown.

Instead of taking the path to the left, which led to the boathouse and playing field, I took the one to the right, which followed a steep, north-facing slope and meandered through a stand of willows and a mix of grass and sunflowers before entering a forest of elms, box elder, and juniper. The long traverse uphill forced me to bend forward and strain to keep Otis secure on my back while he squirmed and rose up and down, as though he wanted a better view.

We didn't stop at the overlook, where I usually cooled off on my way from digging the grave. I was sweating, and Otis's wool sweater made my skin itch. I followed the hard, wind-blown path around the contour of Cemetery Butte and marched up the last stretch of the path and through the knee-high grass to a short wall made from rocks left behind by the glacier. Farmers had probably built the wall centuries ago when they had cleared the fields. I lowered Otis onto a wide flat rock. His breathing was calm now, but mine was hard.

"You were flopping around," I said after my heart slowed down.

"I was imagining myself on a horse, a great warrior riding into battle," Otis said.

"Well, if I'm the horse, I want a better saddle than your scratchy old sweater," I said.

I sat down beside him and took his leathery and wrinkled hand. His fingers were rough and coarse. We didn't speak but stared into the tall grass of the prairie.

The wind atop Cemetery Butte wasn't as strong as the wind outside the cave, perhaps because Cemetery Butte wasn't as high as Windy Butte; its top was flatter, more spread out, better able to absorb the wind. The breeze was just strong enough to counter the sun's intensity and disperse the smell of Otis's sick and unwashed body. After a while, Otis spoke:

"I'm sorry we never built an earthen lodge here, During-the-Event," he said.

I groaned at the sound of my name, the Hidatsa one that Otis had given me to honor my birth during the period of time he called the "Event," when Sammy Goldrausch was murdered and the power was cut off and the government destroyed White Earth River. So I became During-the-Event Pérez. My nickname, D. E., is okay: short, direct. "Hand me the ax, D. E." Nothing complicated about that. I never found out what my parents named me, if they did.

"Well, Silvertooth," I spoke Otis's family name, "you didn't do too badly without an earthen lodge."

"I could've done better. . . . Sammy and I used to come up here to sing and pray," Otis began to recount. "But the others, the old Hidatsa living in town, laughed at me, called me Wannabe, said, 'Show us the blood test, Otis, show us the results.' But really they didn't want to stretch their minds or their mouths or their legs. They preferred the happy services of the Catholics in town. They liked the booming soundtrack, the bright monitor with its easy words, the good feelings that came from standing in a row like corn and praising the rewards of salvation. And the Catholics always had something to eat afterwards. That's why they were fat and couldn't walk up the butte to worship properly."

"Wannabe?" I asked.

"They questioned my ancestry. But what did they know?"

"Lazy sons-of-bitches," I spit out in my best disgust-filled voice.

"And after worship was banned, and Sammy locked up the church, they cowered in their homes, whispering the weak songs about grace. I was the only one who came here, even in the cool season, and danced by myself and wailed so my voice would travel down to Lake Sakakawea. Who was going to arrest me? Sammy was my friend! We chanted together, here up on the butte! Goddamn Tony LePerle!"

Otis's face was orange with rage, but the color quickly faded to yellow, and he slumped forward, worn out, wheezing again. It was always a good story, one of my favorites, about the spiritually empty Hidatsa, and I wanted him to know how much I liked it.

I squeezed his hand. I figured as long as we continued to repeat the story of our existence, he wouldn't die. I looked south, to the juniper, where I had dug Otis's grave near a thick root.

Otis wanted his grave to be oriented in "an east to west direction," so the sun would track straight over his body, ensuring that his spirit felt the sun's warmth from morning to night. This had never made sense to me, but I had humored Otis and bitten my tongue not to ask, "What about in the peak of the cool season when the sun isn't overhead?"

Otis had scattered Malèna's ashes under a thin juniper root, but she was Catholic, not Hidatsa. The other Hidatsa from town were buried in the cemetery, under standard government-issue grave markers. Otis never told me the history of the burial tradition we were following. We had no books about it. Perhaps it wasn't Hidatsa but one that he'd made up as death got closer. "We're going backwards, you know," Otis said. "I'm sorry that we didn't sing together more often so you'd know the old songs better. That was part of my failing," he said.

"You sang in the garden," I said.

"Yes, but maybe that wasn't enough," he said.

I never became accustomed to Otis's singing, the chanting in a distorted voice that resembled crying, the shouting in a strange language that I assumed was Hidatsa but had no way of knowing. Sometimes I struggled to follow along, to imitate the sounds Otis made, but his face, twisted in a painful expression, scared me.

"Did you sing when I was born, Otis?" I asked.

"The basement wasn't a good place for singing."

"What about my mother and father, did they sing?"

"Your father drank a new batch of *tesgüino* and hooted with his friends. I think Tony LePerle was there, goddamn him. Your mother was feeding you."

"Did she give me a name?"

He didn't answer right away.

"Little One. That's what she called you. But she didn't sing. No one sang. I'll sing for your birth, now, if you wish," Otis said.

Little One. Not much better than During-the-Event. And now he wanted to sing about it. How much could be left of a song that had lain unsung in his memory for seventeen-odd years, I wondered? Maybe he'd stumble over the words and give up. I'd be left with a handful of half-sung verses and two dumb names.

But Otis seemed eager to sing. He shifted forward. As he stared at the ground, he mumbled and licked his lips. Before I could say, "Don't bother," he sat upright, contorted his face, and filled his chest with a deep breath. His two arms, extended straight back to the rock wall, supported him. He raised his head to the sky and shouted to the wind.

Oh, Mother Earth and Father Sky, what have we done?
We've brought another one into this sorry world.
He's skinny and small, but we love him so.
How will he survive when we're gone?
Don't hide animals from him.
Send rain and sun for the plants.
And wind to sing him to sleep.
Let him grow tall and strong.
Let him go forth and create.
And bless him, and bless him,

For he is the last as well as the first.
And bless him, and bless him,
For he is the last as well as the first.

When he was finished, he closed his eyes and folded his hands in his lap. His body slumped, and his chest heaved as he drew in air and whistled it out again in a hoarse, gravelly breath. He'd done okay; he'd gotten through it without stopping. Of course, I hadn't expected a happy song, because Otis never sang those. But the words weren't unfamiliar. Otis invoked Mother Earth often during the harvest, thanking her for being generous, although I never noticed a connection between his songs and the growth of the plants. Some years were better than others no matter what we did, or what Otis sang. But "skinny and small"? Was that why my mother called me Little One? Was that how Otis saw me, too? And "go forth and create?" Another garden plot, I guessed. As for being last and first, I supposed Otis meant the only remaining Hidatsa and the first to be born in the town. He was speaking in a vague way, which I attributed to his preoccupation with the spirit life. Something was off, though, and I had a suspicion about what it was.

"That wasn't an old song," I stated.

"No, a new one. I wrote it especially for you," Otis whispered as he breathed slow and steady. I could have thanked him and not pursued my questions, but I pressed on.

"But not when I was born," I said.

"No, recently. Just now, in fact," he answered.

"That's what I thought. You sang in English."

"I can't remember the old one."

"That's okay. I didn't expect you to. This one was fine."

"It's a simple song. Birth songs shouldn't be too complicated."

Otis shifted on the rock. He looked as though he were in pain. "You'll remember the one I taught you to sing when I die, During-the-Event?"

"Yes, Granddad."

I had rehearsed the song for months, tolerating Otis's coaching on the proper vocalizations and phrasing until finally, impatient, I had refused to practice it anymore.

"You promise?"

"I won't forget it."

"I'll believe you. Now show me my grave."

He was able to walk the short distance to the grave, with the support of my arm to steady him and bear part of his weight. We stood together and looked down into the hole. He leaned against me, an arm resting on my shoulder.

I had planned the cuts in the earth to do the least amount of damage to the roots of the juniper and had managed to save the thin feeder roots, which remained suspended in air between the walls of the grave. At first Otis didn't say anything, and I worried that he was estimating the depth of the grave. I had started digging it a few days before, but a tough layer of yellow-orange clay had slowed me down. I had to use the pick to break up the earth. And then I'd taken the morning off to go sailing.

Finally, Otis spoke in a whisper: "It's very deep. You've done a good job. I can see it was a lot of work."

At least an arm's length short of your specifications, I thought.

"But it's a sad end to life, even though this is the proper way to be buried, the most useful to nature, the only way my spirit will join my wife's," Otis said.

His eyebrows were squeezed together so two deep furrows formed. Abruptly, he relaxed them.

"You'll keep my clothes, remember, so you'll have an extra set. And my sheet, too, even though it's old and the tradition is to be buried wrapped in it."

"Yes, Granddad," I reassured him, although I had no intention of undressing Otis and placing him naked in the ground without protection from the worms, insects, and moles that could tunnel through the soil. He'd go to the grave in the jeans and red-and-black-and-white flannel shirt he was wearing. We had pulled these from a house two seasons ago.

"You want to go back to the cave now, Otis?" I asked. He was wobbling, leaning more and more against me, grasping my shoulder more tightly.

"You're forgetting about my wife," he said.

"I'm sorry. We can visit her grave, too."

"Haven't I taught you anything?"

A sharp sound rushed from Otis's mouth. I thought he was starting to cry, then his laughter filled the air.

"I have to make sure she gets ready for me!"

Otis's foul breath almost made me choke, but I smiled anyway, relieved that he wasn't crying, but unsure of what he found so funny. His laughter degenerated into a spell of coughing. After he'd calmed down, he untied the faded red ribbon that secured his long braid.

"I want you to tie a prayer ribbon on the limb above her grave," he said and handed me the ribbon.

I rubbed the smooth material between my fingers. Otis had bound his hair with it for as long as I could remember, sometimes in a loose ponytail, then once I learned to weave, in a braid.

We made a jagged path through the grass to the juniper. While Otis clung to my belt, I knotted the ribbon to a sprig of juniper

19

leaves. The ribbon was almost gray, and the loose tails of the knot almost blended in with the bluish leaves of the juniper.

"That will be a sign for her and a marker for me, to help me find her, my wife."

"I'm sure you will."

I tried to imagine Otis as a spirit, traveling up the roots of the juniper. I had seen plants decay in the compost pile and the bones of animals bleach in the sun and had found the bones of humans dusty and broken in the rubble of the town. But where were their spirits? If I couldn't see the spirits of the animals that lived in the butte, why did I think that I'd be able to see Otis's? I wanted to believe that his would look like one of the thin, long fibers attached to the morels that I dug from mats of leaves in the forest. Something that I could touch and hold.

Otis interrupted my thoughts: "I'm so weak. Maybe you should leave me here, save yourself the trip after I die."

"No, you need something to eat, that's all. We'll stop at the garden. The lettuce isn't so bitter this year."

"I'd like some meat."

A snare I had set on a game trail in a clearing near a box elder thicket had been tripped, and hanging from the wire loop was a rabbit. I stroked its soft fur and felt its chest. It was not warm, and the limbs were resistant to movement; yet no flies buzzed over the dried blood on its nose. Maybe early that morning? I guessed at how long it had been dead. Was its spirit inside, or had it already gone to the butte, or somewhere else? I didn't say a prayer of thanks but gutted the rabbit, buried the organs, and carried the animal back to the garden by its legs. The rabbit was big enough for a meal.

Otis had fallen off the bench and lay curled on his side, as though he had dropped from the sky. From a distance he appeared to be dead, but up close I saw his chest rising and falling. The years of working and living outside hadn't prevented his black hair from turning gray or his body from shriveling up so his clothes hung from him like thick loose skin. I sat down beside him and placed my hand on his shoulder.

"We trapped a rabbit, Granddad, a good size one," I said.

Otis opened his eyes but didn't move.

"I was thinking about your father. The time he was feeding a deer corn out of his hand near the gardens. When the deer stretched its neck to eat, he slipped a rope around it. The deer bolted and he fell down, and the deer pulled him across the fields. When the deer paused, he jumped up, laughing. The deer took off and knocked him off balance again. Finally, he circled around a tree so the rope would hold it. As the deer struggled, neighbors came running with clubs. Then we built a fire in the playing field and roasted it, with garlic and rosemary. Everyone was there, your mother, father, me, you, all our neighbors. The meat was very tasty."

"That's what my father was like?"

This was the only story, full story, really, that Otis ever told me about my father.

Otis sat up and smiled. "Javier drank too much, but he was very funny. Always joking. Never mean."

I imagined standing in the meadow, near the river, watching my father be towed by the panicked deer. I wished I had been the one to witness this.

"I'm ready to go home now. We'll have the rabbit," Otis said.

At the entrance to the cave, in the belly of the clay stove, I laid a nest of dried grass and twigs and brought it to smoke with my bow and stick. When it flared, I blew on the flame to ignite the pieces of split driftwood, which crackled and caught. The fire was alive, and I hovered over it, absorbing its heat and not backing off when sparks popped toward my face. I unfolded my wooden chair, the one I had rubbed with the purple juice of June berries to distinguish it from Otis's dirty-yellow chair, and settled onto the wobbly seat.

After a while, when the fire had died down to a thick bed of coals, I set the oven grate, which I had extracted from a mangled stove in the town's ruins, on top and weighted one corner with a rock to steady it. Into the rabbit's flesh I rubbed garlic from the garden and sagebrush I had collected from a field beyond the broken wind turbines and crystals of salt that I had found on the edges of a dried-up pond. The fatty skin sizzled and sputtered. I breathed in the greasy air.

During my years in White Earth River, rabbit was my favorite animal: easy to trap, kill, and clean; the fur, once enough skins were tanned, made a warm blanket or coat; and one plump adult was just enough for two people.

I helped Otis walk from his bed across the willow mats to the front of the cave. Instead of seating him at the table, I lowered him against a cottonwood post, the one with the notches marking the seasons, until he was on the floor. I preferred sitting on the floor to eat; Otis's legs were too stiff to bend very much so they stuck out straight in front of him. The notches on the post, including the most recent one I had made to mark the end of the cool season, rose above Otis's head. There were twenty-eight notches, one for each season that we lived in the cave. I started to make them sometime before I learned to read, when I began using a knife, around what I guess was age three or four.

"You'll need rope, a lot of rope," Otis blurted out, with a force-fulness that startled me. His plate almost fell from his lap.

"What?" I said. "What are you talking about?"

I leaned toward him and steadied his plate.

"Yellow rope. And pulleys, too," he said. "You'll have to scav-enge those. A block and tackle, if you can find it."

"Block and tackle?" I tore dark meat off a rabbit leg with my teeth. I loved the greasy taste of its legs and thighs.

"Volume one, or maybe two," Otis said.

He was referring to the *Encyclopedia of Simple and Not So Simple Machines*. When I was young, he had read the three volumes to me, but often I didn't pay attention to the descriptions of mechanical de-vices. I preferred *The Child's Compendium of Story and Verse*, a book Otis found impractical, a waste of time, which was surprising, given his own interest in stories as a way to justify his life.

"What about the orange rope?" I asked. We had a coil of that in the cart down in the garden. I pulled the other leg from the carcass and began eating it with both hands, as though I were eating an ear of corn.

"The ancestors specified yellow, During-the-Event. A continu-ous thread of yellow, from the cave to the juniper."

"When did they say that?" I asked, my mouth full, as I chewed the meat. "You never told me this."

"The yellow will help me find my wife."

"Are you going to eat your rabbit?" He hadn't touched it.

"A few more bites."

A continuous thread of . . . off-hand inventions, that's what the ancestors seemed to have specified. And this latest addition to the burial plan—sprung on me in the middle of eating roast rabbit!—I wanted to ignore, although I knew this wasn't a choice, that it would require a trip to the ruins to scrounge for rope. But not yet. First, I cracked open a femur and sucked the sweet marrow from the bone.

"You'll remember the knots?" Otis asked me.

"Don't worry."

"Wait until I'm nice and stiff. That'll give you plenty of leverage. And remember, my body mustn't touch the ground until I'm in the grave."

"I'll remember."

It was a fanciful plan, trussing up Otis's body with yellow rope, setting a block and tackle and pulleys, and hoisting his corpse across the valley, one that would have taken me days to rig, if I knew how, using equipment I would never find in the ruins. How long would the rope have to be? At least a kilometer, maybe two. Otis seemed to believe he could fly to his grave like a spirit, with, of course, mechanical assistance. I took his plate and ate his portion of rabbit.

"Yellow rope. Okay," I said, unfolding my legs and standing up. I dropped our plates in the wash pail. I left the rabbit carcass, with a thigh and leg remaining, for later, and covered it with a cloth to keep away the flies.

"Check by the back door. In the storage room," Otis said. "There's always yellow rope there."

"Where do you want to wait? On the floor or in the bed?"

"Right here, but I'd like the pillows."

I covered him with a patched cotton blanket and wedged behind his back the two feather pillows I had made from geese I'd netted on the playing field.

"If you have to go, use this," I said and placed a plastic bucket beside him.

"I'm not doing that anymore."

"Oh, yes, you are. You just ate, remember?"

I scrambled down the flanks of the butte and traversed to the right, to the perimeter road on the edge of the town site. The overgrown grid of dirt streets was littered with the debris of collapsed homes, much of it now buried in the weeds and grass.

On the night the town was destroyed, the heavy machines passed through the rows of flimsy prefabricated houses like harvesters reaping an unwanted crop. The machines' steel treads compressed and churned up the earth. Their wide blades and scoops leveled homes and flattened the community center, Catholic church, food distribution annex, clinic, and government representative's office. They spared the old oak tree, which marked what had been the center of the town and was now only accessible by following a jumble of paths lined with thistles and cottonwood saplings. Thistles hadn't grown in the town before the machines arrived, Otis had told me.

I followed an overgrown lumpy tread to the house that Otis and my parents had once lived in and where I was born and spent the first five months of my life. Unlike the other houses in the town, ours was never completely demolished. Perhaps the machine operator had been hasty, or bored, and had only swiped at the house with the long arm of his machine. Maybe he'd said to himself, "Good enough," and had left the house to sag and split apart on its own.

A portion of one wall still stood: a plane of colors—early spring green, robin's egg blue, and goldenrod yellow—rising from what must have been the living room up through the stairwell and into the upstairs. I wondered if my parents had slept up there and me with them.

Staring at the wrecked house upset my stomach.

This hadn't always been the case. When I was a child, the destroyed town had had no significance to me. I had had no knowledge of what the town had been or awareness that I had been born and lived there with parents who then disappeared. The town was just a place that contained "buried treasure," as Otis would refer to our finds of clothes, furniture, tools, dishes, and an occasional book. It was just a jumbled up and broken place that we sometimes walked through on our way to and from the cave, and sometimes a place to which Otis would abruptly shuffle me from the garden and down into our house's basement. Was he evading agents, left-behind people, wanderers looking for food? He never said.

In fact, had Otis been able to keep the tragedy of the Event to himself, and not named me after it, I would never have questioned him about my parents. If he'd spoken only about our life in the garden and the cave, or hadn't spoken at all but simply grunted at me, I would have remained ignorant of the Event.

I felt my stomach bloat and press against the leather belt holding up my shorts. My bowels were turning. I dropped my pants and squatted.

Otis only spoke a few times of the continental disaster that coincided with the destruction of White Earth River: the massacre of old, sick, hungry, displaced, unskilled, and undesirable people. When government agents entered White Earth River with their machines, they were seeking revenge for Sammy Goldrausch's murder, but also for an easy way to dispose of a handful of old people and a few of their adult children living in a co-housing retirement project in the country. Two birds with one stone. Another town off the list.

"When the seas took New York, that's when we started to shut down," Otis would say. "The diplomats came home, government recalled the military, international trade stopped. No one could have predicted how fast life would deteriorate, not even the men and women whose jobs it was to predict these kinds of things."

The United States merged with Canada to control the resources of the North American continent. Then the two powers decided they had to include Mexico, too, because the Mexican border was too long to patrol. "With all the unwanted people, you'd think the government could've extended the metal border fence with a human one to keep out intruders. But what government in its right mind would pass out rifles to millions of idle, hungry people?" Otis would ask. "It would be like Tony LePerle, only on a larger scale."

Canada and the United States decided to site the capital, the Center, in the geographic center of North America—Rugby, North Dakota—to emphasize their dominance over Mexico. I guess Otis was lucky to be living in Bismarck; work in the Center offered him protection from what went on elsewhere.

Even with only three countries to govern, there were still too many people to feed. The government adopted a policy of population assessment, relocation, and culling—what Otis said was a fancy word for slaughter. The rich, smart, and lucky found places in industrial, manufacturing, or agricultural preserves; or in institutions, like schools and hospitals; or in the military on bases spread over the continent; or in one of the regional cities or the capital, the Center. The government ran everything.

Some people tried to retreat into clusters and live off stored provisions, but once they ate all their canned food, they had to search for more. They joined the waves of migrants fighting over food and water as they made their way inland from the flooded coasts. Some of these people were government rejects, others had fallen through the cracks and were never classified. They became stranded along highways, on foot and in vehicles, out of water, food, and gas, with no idea of where they were going, "just inland." "Now the government had them where it wanted them, all together like that," Otis would say. "Of course, natural attrition killed a lot. But the military's flame cannons took care of the rest. Incinerated them. Cars burned for days. Tony LePerle saw some of the remains," Otis would recount. I suppose Otis was in White Earth River, then, with Malèna, before she died.

I stepped over a scattered pile of white moldy siding and weathered gray trim to the door of the storage room. It had been built as an addition to the back of the house and, like the wall leading to my parents' upstairs bedroom, was still standing. Otis had cleared out his tools years ago. There wasn't any yellow rope on the floor or hanging on the wall; I doubt if there ever was.

I remembered a coil of rope, white rope, with blue-and-white plastic rings on it, in the corner of the boathouse, beneath the rack of blue life preservers. This would have to do, I thought.

I walked east through town and crossed the White Earth River on the footbridge. At the junction of paths leading to Cemetery Butte and the playing field, I took the left fork and followed the river toward the narrow white sand beach where Otis and I bathed. The boathouse was at one end of the beach, with a dock extending out its back door. Up from the beach was the old soccer field where, as the town was being shut down, people had built fires and roasted game. Once the town's people had disappeared, a flock of geese took over the field. They avoided the area by the soccer goal posts, where charred wood from the fires lay: they must've known that other animals had been slaughtered and cooked there.

The metal wheels rattled in their track as I lifted the door of the boathouse.

I had remembered the rope as white and was prepared to tell Otis that it was all I could find but was relieved that the rope was yellow after all. Otis would be happy; at least this part of his burial plan would be realized.

"Yellow rope," I said and dropped it on the willow mat and handed Otis a bight. "I found it in the boathouse."

Otis rolled the shiny rope between his thumb and finger.

"I don't like the feel of this," he said. "Too slick. Knots won't hold. It's better that we use the orange rope. Why did you waste your time looking for this?"

I took the end of the rope from him and threw the coil across the floor.

"It's yellow. It's always good to have yellow rope around," I said.

"I guess so. I'm a little hungry."

I made a soup with the rest of the rabbit plus a few carrots and onions and a handful of mashed garlic cloves. Instead of walking Otis to the front of the cave to eat, as I had earlier in the day, I let him sit up in bed, his back supported by the junipers. As before, I sat on the floor, with my own back pushing up against my bed frame, and faced Otis.

"Do you feel it?" Otis asked after he'd sipped a spoonful of soup.

"No, not really," I said.

He was speaking of death. He spoke of it as though it were a visitor he was eager to welcome into the cave. I chewed the soft ribs of the rabbit. A few bands of flesh were still attached.

"Hmm . . . So you don't feel it, then?" he asked.

"No, I guess not," I said.

What I felt was the waiting, for another revision of the burial plan, for one more day.

"Well it's there. In the air. A disturbance. I've only sensed this a few times in my life . . . when Malèna passed."

"I don't know what happens when it comes, Otis. Maybe your heart just stops beating, like the animals we kill. Maybe that's all. Maybe there's nothing more."

"They have spirits, too."

I didn't want to argue about the existence of spirits. Or the signs of impending death. The carrots, I noticed, could have been simmered a little longer.

"When we were up on the butte, I began to worry that my spirit isn't strong enough to join Malèna's. That I'm so weak and thin I won't be of much use to the tree. Or Malèna. Then I began to think about you, how I hadn't taught you everything you needed to know. That I'd forgotten something, but I couldn't remember what it was . . ."

His voice broke. I didn't like it when he sounded so mournful.

"I know all I need to know," I said. "I planted the garden by myself this season, remember. And you're eating the rabbit tonight. You're not going to die anytime soon."

"No, there was something . . ."

"It'll come to you."

I couldn't fathom knowing more than I did. Our life was simple. We got up in the morning and worked in the garden, we ate vegetables and trapped or caught and killed game, we talked to pass the time, we read the few books we had, sometimes I wandered off on my own, we slept when darkness arrived. That was the extent of our life. It had a rhythm, which I had mastered.

Otis began coughing, and I took away his bowl and stood ready to slap his back if he started choking. But he didn't. The coughing stopped. I waited until he was breathing steadily and then went to the front of the cave for another helping of soup and the asparagus leftover from the day before. As I lowered myself to the floor again and crossed my legs, Otis started to speak.

"When your mother and father went to the playing field that night, when the machines came, the air was unsettled, too," he said. "The men always hung the deer from the soccer goal posts before they staked it out to roast. Everyone was happy, together in front of the fire, drinking your father's *tesgüino*. But I was too tired to go along that evening, and your mother asked me to take care of you. I brought you down into the basement. It was quiet there, like the cave. But the air wasn't right."

I stopped eating and looked at him. My parents went to the playing fields that night? My mother asked him to take care of me? Wait a minute, I thought, they weren't *supposed* to appear in our story.

"Later, the basement walls started vibrating. For a long time, two hours at least," Otis said. "I couldn't make heads or tails of it. I thought it might be an earthquake, and I tried to remember, when had there ever been an earthquake in North Dakota? Then the vibrating got louder. The basement was shaking. An engine was groaning. Steel treads were clanking against the ground. I could smell the diesel. I thought it was on top of us and waited for the ceiling to collapse. Metal clanked against metal. A huge weight slammed into our house. The framing ripped. Nails screeched as they let loose. Our house was coming down. I thought we'd be crushed and I got down on my knees and held you and prayed to God. I was never religious, never went to church, but there I was praying to Malèna's god. I didn't think it would come to this. Arrest and relocation maybe. But destruction? That was a surprise."

At first I thought he was joking, introducing these new twists into our story to keep me entertained. The part about dropping to his knees to pray to a Catholic god especially made me want to laugh. But he wasn't grinning or smiling. His eyes were bulging wide open.

He licked his lips and opened his mouth wide to suck in air. I'd never seen him so terrified.

"At most I thought there'd be some warning shots to herd us into trucks for arrest and relocation. But demolition? Whew! That was a surprise!"

He chuckled and then hawked up and swallowed some phlegm. The damp sour air that we shared settled over me and made the hair on my skin stand up. I set my half-empty soup bowl on the willow floor and studied Otis's sallow face for a clue to what he might say next. He squirmed against the juniper wall as though ants were crawling over his skin.

"I thought it was heavy trucks! A police action. A display of force. Some arrests. But murder and destruction. Whew! That was a surprise!"

"My parents were there? Your vision . . . I thought . . ."

"You always liked bedtime stories."

"And you liked telling them!"

Otis's knees fell to the side, and he shifted again, struggling to stay upright. For a moment he lost his balance and extended an arm to keep from falling forward. He coughed again.

"Oh, you cried all the time, missed your mother's tit!" he moaned. "Your parents came home drunk. Hollered in their bedroom. I kept you in the basement with me. I slept better down there."

Then he bent toward me and confided in a wheezy whisper: "Bunch of old people. A few young men with rifles. What threat were we?"

"Wait a minute, Otis. You said my parents . . ."

"Oh, gardening was women's work. All that talking. It never stopped. Digging a basement, I became a man again!" he bellowed.

"Otis, what are you talking about?" I cried out.

"Things got worse before they got better. Only one diaper for you to mess up. Had to let you go naked on the bottom. A couple of times I thought about letting you die, just to shut you up. I was so lonely, no one to talk to, and all you could do was cry. I started singing and reading out loud. Anything to drown you out, make me feel less alone. Thankfully, you learned to speak early on."

"You *knew* where they were?"

"I hated it. That night. End of everything."

"Why didn't you *warn* them?"

"I was so scared. And then the nightmares came. Luckily you slept through those."

"Why didn't you go out and bring them to the basement?"

"I didn't want us to live like savages, like the rest of the continent. I wanted us to be free, to live a pure life. With respect for humans and in harmony with nature. Like before the white people. When the Indians lived here."

"You mean your ancestors?"

He gazed beyond me and focused on the wall of the cave.

"I was very sad when Malèna died. And now I'm leaving you," he said.

I thought he would cry. He disgusted me.

"Yeah, well, don't worry," I said. "I can gather and trap. I know how to swim and paddle and sail the canoe, too. I've gone all the way to White Earth Bay and am going to sail even farther."

"Oh, I did a lot of dumb things when I was young, too. And you'll do a lot more before you grow up," he said and started rubbing his back against the juniper trunks, as though he were scratching a bite, unmoved by my boasting. Then he flattened his eyes in a slit of concentration and stared at me.

"You need a wife," he said in a matter-of-fact way.

"A wife? A wife?" I started to laugh. I slapped my thigh and hooted. Death was making him crazy. Or maybe living with a lie for so long had finally cracked him up.

"I had a lot of girls before I met Malèna. I enjoyed them all, but not as much as your grandmother. You'll see. A strong young man like you will have his choice."

His wheezing filled the silence in the cave. I thought he had said all he'd wanted to say and would settle into sleep. But instead he cleared his throat and hawked. He pointed a finger at me: "You're more of a son to me than a grandson. You were the only child I ever raised. Maria was grown when I met her, already married to Javier. She wasn't my child. She was Malèna's daughter. I didn't know her very well."

"She wasn't related to you?"

"No, but I didn't care about that. They were good people, Javier and Maria. But they shouldn't have come to White Earth River. I could take care of Malèna better than Maria could, and I didn't need them to take care of me after Malèna died. They should've stayed in Bismarck."

He spoke as though he were talking about the morning clouds and what shape they would take by afternoon.

"They were on the playing field."

"Hmm."

"We could've warned them. They could've been with us."

"Funny how these things work out."

I felt the lattice of willows pressing into my bottom. Nothing existed except the foul air at the back of the cave.

"I don't have your blood, then, only my parents' blood."

Otis ignored me.

"I never knew my father," he continued. "He left my mother when I was an infant. She was a white, but Sammy convinced me that my father might have been Hidatsa. He said we'd get a blood test, prove it. Sammy knew a lot about the Hidatsa, how they had lived along the Missouri. He'd read their history and whatnot, knew more than the handful of old Hidatsa and Mandan and Arikara living in our retirement village. He taught me how to preserve seeds, which plants had the most nutritional value. We wanted to return to another time, one before there was a government. When the Event happened, I thought a prophecy was coming true, even though Sammy didn't live to join us in this future."

"You're not Hidatsa, then. And I'm not either."

"You've been Hidatsa almost since you were born. It doesn't matter that you don't have my blood or even that you don't like to sing. You're my son."

"No. Our blood isn't right. None of it is."

"You're my son."

"Are we whites, Otis?"

Otis slouched against the wall and stared straight ahead at the juniper trunks—not at me. His hair was loose, falling down around his shoulders. His face seemed to have become softer and fuller from his confession. Although his skin had kept its yellow tint, it didn't seem as leathery and tough as it had earlier in the day. His wrinkles seemed to have filled in. He looked younger. In a way, and this may have been the dim light playing tricks on me, he looked more like a woman than a man.

A few minutes later, he lowered himself to the bed and began to snore.

I stirred the coals in the clay stove and added pieces of driftwood and waited for them to pop and flare. Fat on the stove grate melted and dripped into the fire. Smoke curled toward the roof of the cave. I breathed in the greasy fumes.

It was dark in the cave now, except for the fire. To light up the cave, I propped the piece of mirror against the clay chimney so light from the flames was reflected into the room.

In the dim light I began pacing, quietly rummaging through the few belongings we had, searching for an account of what had happened the night the machines had come or of his "conversion" to Hidatsa, notes or a diary that Otis had written during those first lonely days, perhaps hidden among the sheaves of paper on the shelf: planting schedules, my writing and arithmetic exercises, sketches of the valley from the cave. Or in one of Otis's dresser drawers (he had two, as did I), tucked behind a shirt or pair of jeans. Or in the wooden stand between our beds where he kept the black book of photographs.

I found no written record in any of these places, only the book of photographs in the wooden stand. And although the images were old, I hoped they would give me some clue to how Otis's mind worked, a glimpse into why he'd gone to the trouble of creating the story about his phony vision.

Many of the photographs had faded to brown and white, and some were torn and creased, but at least they proved that certain moments of Otis's past had occurred as he said they had; the tattered paper evidence couldn't be altered.

I sat on the willow mat, across from Otis, with the album opened on my lap. If I tipped the pages at the right angle, I could see the images. I wondered: What would it be like to stand in front of the tall buildings in the photographs, to kneel in front of the statues in parks, or to sit at tables arranged with platters of food as I smiled and held hands with a woman like the one in the photo, Otis's wife, Malèna? Would I be as handsome as Otis in dark pants with a crease down the front of them, a white shirt, and a dark coat? Would I cut my hair short and slick it back with grease or water? And my wife, would she be as tall as Malèna was standing on her toes in black shoes with thin high heels? Would my wife's hair be long and dark and tied in a ponytail that hung to her waist? Would she wear a tight-fitting, pale dress with buttons up the front that sparkled like stars and a wide shiny belt that cinched her waist? Or a long, white lace dress that covered her feet? Would my wife clutch a handful of flowers?

Otis had told me stories about his working days, when he led a crew that built office and residential towers in Rugby, North Dakota, during the first wave of construction in the creation of the continent's new capital city, the Center. I remembered the names of the men on the crew, who in one photo stood in a line with Otis. All were dressed in heavy work clothes. They stood perched on a beam, with arms around each other, those on the ends holding onto vertical risers for balance. Behind them in the distance, metal and glass buildings glistened in the sun. "To Otis, number one. Working with you has been an 'express' ride to the top every time! Best wishes for a happy retirement." Below the message on yellowing paper was a row of signatures.

His crew had named Otis after an elevator because he worked fast and pushed them to do the same, which was why they did well in the Center, why Otis could afford to wear fancy clothes and take Malèna to restaurants where there was never a shortage of food.

I had been cultivating around a hill of corn the first time I had called Otis by his nickname. "Hey, Otis, give me that trowel," I had said. "Here you go, number three," Otis had chuckled, using the endearment he reserved for joking with his men to let them know he was boss.

After that, I had stopped calling him Granddaddy. And Otis was much easier to say than Johnny Silvertooth, his full name. He seemed to like being reminded of his life as the head of a team of ironworkers racing to build the new capital of the North American continent.

But this life, his working years when he and Malèna were young, had money, and went out to restaurants, was a different time, one in which the new continental government was forming: abandoning the coasts, the southeast, and much of the southwest; moving desirable people inland to regional cities, mapping out industrial and agricultural preserves. Perhaps at first Otis believed the government's lies about its adapting to a hotter climate and building a continent for the future. Being isolated in the interior on the edge of a productive agricultural region might have convinced him the government was to be trusted, that his work in building the Center was noble. The White Earth River co-housing retirement project would also help him think all was going according to a plan, which was why he probably cursed Tony LePerle so much: he exposed the government's brutal policy of culling and wrecked the arrangement Otis and the other retirees had. How could Otis ignore what the government was doing and think that he'd escape it?

The photos of Malèna and Otis offered no hints about what might have led Otis, that night when the machines came, to choose our life rather than some other one. The photos only honored his life with Malèna. I wish I had one or two photos that documented our survival in White Earth River, from the time before Otis's confession, before our life started to end. Of course, I couldn't have known that it would end so quickly. And, we didn't have a camera.

Otis coughed and mumbled something. I closed the black book of photographs. He opened his eyes slowly and stared down at me.

"That's just a glimpse," he said. "A life that was old when I made the record of it. Must've been the late thirties. Twenty-forty-five was when I retired."

Otis rolled on his side and faced me.

"Sometimes I miss that life. There'll be no restaurants in the juniper."

There aren't any here, either, I thought. I thumbed through the pages of photographs until I found the one of a brick house.

"My mother and father lived here," I stated.

"No," Otis said, without looking at the photograph. "That's where Malèna and I lived in Bismarck. Maria had moved out before I met Malèna. Ours was a late-in-life marriage . . . Tortas of all types— rice, pear, nut, ricotta, chocolate. The ricotta were my favorite. So sweet. I don't know which went first, her heart or her lungs. We went to the hospital together, on the train, but I came home with only a handful of ashes and a piece of bone. That's all Government gave me. I dug a small hole, not like the deep one you've dug for me. But I worry that the heat of the oven destroyed her spirit or that I'll have to struggle to find her. You know, she's spoken to me."

"Yes, that's what you said."

I believed this because I wanted to think he'd speak to me and fill the silent world that he'd warned me would come when he died. I looked at him, expecting to see a mournful expression, but he was smiling. His eyes sparkled as though he were savoring a private joke.

"She was so beautiful. Exotic. Full of life. Most of all I've missed sleeping with her, her head on my shoulder. Even if we hadn't been together all day or spoken a word or had an argument, sleeping en- twined like that reunited us. And sometimes we would make love. That's what I'll do after I die, in the juniper. It's up to me to find her."

Make love. The expression jumped out at me, as kissing had earlier in the day. Otis had never used those words, make love, before.

"You'll find her," I said, "You were always able to track animals."

"Yes, and you'll be lucky, too. You'll meet someone to love, like I did. Then your rooster will crow and your wife will scream with pleasure. I'll hear you singing of your happiness. I'll see your children running in the garden."

Bismarck, White Earth River, the spirit life: Otis was floating back and forth, remembering what had happened and make believing about what would never happen: A wife. Children. I barked a short laugh over his expression "rooster." I knew he was referring to the penis, although he had never before used a nickname for either his or mine. And the crowing bit: Did he know that sometimes at night as I slept and dreamed my penis grew large? I waited for Otis to say more, but he only sighed and rolled onto his back.

I studied the photographs again and tried to imagine the life he and Malèna had shared, the moments of tenderness and secrecy that Otis had alluded to but had never spoken of so openly. Each had pursued his own life, Otis as ironworker and then as town . . . what?— digging a basement seemed to be his greatest accomplishment—and Malèna as baker in her parents' business and then leader in the town's Catholic church. But they had had a special, secret life together, too. I tried to imagine how White Earth River would have been different if Malèna hadn't died before I was born. How she would have treated me like a son, or a grandson, as Otis did. How she would have prepared our meals. She was probably a better cook than Otis or me. Would we all have slept at the back of the cave together? Would she and Otis have lain in his bed entwined on the cornhusk mattress and made love while I slept in the bed across from them?

"Make love" was a funny expression, like other "make" expressions, make tea, make noise, make sense, but different, I knew, a private expression for something that only Otis and Malèna could do, lying close together and probably touching and kissing. The other expression, "scream with pleasure," I hated. Why would I want to make my wife scream with pleasure? It reminds me of "scream with terror," which is what I imagine Otis and my parents did over the sound of the clanking machines.

I was tired of looking at the photographs and couldn't wait until morning for Otis to answer my question, so I tried to wake him up. "Granddad, what's make love?" I asked. Otis didn't answer. I could hear fluid gurgling in his lungs, a wheezy breath coming out of his mouth. I closed the black book of photographs and watched his chest rise and fall.

In the gray-blue light of morning, I lay on the cornhusk mattress, a goose-feather pillow flat under my head, and listened for Otis's breathing. I couldn't hear it and couldn't see his chest rising under the folds of the rabbit-skin blanket.

I got up and walked over and unfastened a button on his flannel shirt. His heartbeat was weak. His chest didn't seem to be rising; then suddenly he gulped for air. When I tried to sit him up, to help him breathe, he moaned a long "Nooo . . ."

I pressed my hand against his cheek. It was cool.

"You didn't eat enough rabbit last night and now you're getting cold."

I smoothed the soft fur of the blanket, snugged it up around his neck, and tucked it under his shoulders.

"You want some tea? I can start a fire and make some."

I waited for an answer, but Otis didn't speak.

"No? Okay. Maybe later."

I knew what I had to do. At the beginning of the previous warm season, I had lain with Otis on a deerskin in the garden at night to scare off the birds and rabbits that tried to steal seeds and munch on the new shoots. We had spooned together, Otis's body warming mine throughout the night. Now, it was my turn to offer the same comfort to him. I touched his cheek and thought of the thin draft that reached our beds, the dampness that seeped from the earth through the wall of junipers.

"You remember lying together, Otis, in the garden?"

I slid under the rabbit-skin blanket and nuzzled against him, spread a leg and an arm over him, pulled him close to me and smelled his sick body—urine, feces, phlegm. He relaxed and emitted little grunts and moans. I tried to make out what he was trying to say, but none of the sounds formed into words that I could understand. He took my hand, and we fell asleep.

I woke up some time later, midmorning. Sunlight edged into the cave. I had rolled to the outside, away from Otis. He was still on his back but had straightened both arms down along his sides. I slipped my hand inside his shirt and touched his cool dry skin. There wasn't a heartbeat. A surge of panic flooded me: I had failed to keep him warm.

I climbed on top of him and pulled the rabbit-skin blanket around us so the heat from my body and my hot breath, trapped under the quilt of rabbit pelts, could revive him.

He didn't stir, and after a few minutes I pushed myself away, terrified, and studied the yellow skin of his face. It had acquired a greenish-blue cast, as had his scalp, giving his white hair a greenish tinge as well. His mouth was frozen open in the shape of an "O." His teeth were bared as though his last words had been painful and lodged in his throat, suffocating him. I had failed to keep him warm.

I whipped my bow and stick until smoke and then fire filled the stove. I added driftwood until a blaze leapt up the chimney. I stoked the fire until dampness fled the air, the timbers of the cave creaked from the heat, and the insects and spiders hiding against the cool earth behind the junipers began to fall to the floor. Sweat ran down my arms and chest. I set my chair beside Otis's bed and watched his still body for motion, wondering what he had been trying to say when he last exhaled. Something about his wife? Something about make love? I gripped the edge of the chair until my damp palms turned purple from the June berry stain. The cave took on the atmosphere that had accompanied our lapses in conversation, our silences.

Perhaps it was the dimness at the back of the cave or the creases of the rabbit-skin blanket, but as I scanned Otis's body, I thought I saw his chest rising and falling. Was this his spirit leaving his body, already starting its journey to search for Malèna?

"Are you ready, Otis? Do you want me to take you down?" I asked him.

I began pacing. The low ceiling of the cave seemed to bear down on me, and I ducked as though the timbers were falling. I touched my drawings in the soot on the ceiling, the stick figures of men and animals that I had made in childhood. What was I doing? Otis's spirit was flying around the cave, struggling to find its way out, and I was trying to avoid it, dipping down when it came too close. In the piece of mirror resting on the dresser and propped against the wall I saw it, there in the glass: dark streaks painted on a brown face, black eyes, a long nose.

"Otis!" I shouted, and then recognized my hands in the reflection, touching the greasy smears and June berry stains on my cheeks.

By the middle of the following day, Otis's corpse had begun to rot, and the green-headed flies arrived, attracted to the fluids that he had released when his muscles relaxed. This same type of fly buzzed over my feces in the woods. I hated them and their vicious noise. I wouldn't let them land on Otis. The only way to protect him was to wrap his body in the deerskin.

I dragged him to the front of the cave and unfolded the large skin that we had sewn from several hides and used to cover the cave's entrance in the cool season. I spread it over the willow mats and aligned Otis near the center, then, after waving my arms to clear the air of flies, threw a flap over Otis and rolled him up into a tight bundle. The orange rope was in the broken cart in the garden along with the tools; the yellow one would have to do. I tied a bowline with a long tail so the slippery rope wouldn't come unknotted and fed the other end of the rope through the loop. I folded excess deerskin over Otis's feet and another flap over his head and then wound the yellow rope around him, finishing the job with four half-hitches. The flies couldn't penetrate this cocoon and soon departed.

The bundle was too heavy and awkward to carry, so I towed Otis outside the cave to the ledge and pushed him over the lip. He started to slide along the steep sandstone slab of the butte, then stopped, snagged on a rock protrusion. After a moment, as though he were deciding whether or not to continue, the bundle rolled free until a sandstone pedestal, a hoodoo, stopped it. I scrambled down the butte and jockeyed it loose. With a light tap of my foot, Otis continued his journey, twisting, bumping, and tumbling toward the grassy terrace. Near the bottom the rope caught again, and Otis pivoted and wedged into a crack.

I imagined the spirits of the animals we had trapped and eaten, the deer, rabbits, birds, and fish, stirring inside this fracture in the butte, wondering what was blocking their exit. I inched down the slope and whipped the free end of the rope, sending Otis on to the terrace, where he rolled to a stop. The yellow rope had loosened, some of the strands were cut, and the deerskin was abraded. If I had used only a single wrap, the bundle would have come unraveled and Otis would be lying before me, cut up and broken.

I wanted to haul him up Cemetery Butte as fast as possible, so I fashioned a harness from the excess rope, with loops that I could slip my bare arms through. The weight of his body pulled at my back, and the rope cut into my flesh. The sound of the deerskin flattening stalks of flowers, bumping along hillocks of grass, crunching over the dirt and stones of the road, and catching and releasing on the knotholes of the footbridge's planking tortured me.

At the trail junction to Cemetery Butte, I wiped sweat off my chest and brow and massaged the red indentations on my shoulders. Thick clouds and the close, moist air at least protected me from the sun.

It had been easier carrying Otis up Cemetery Butte on my back, and as I panted and leaned into the last steep section before I hauled him over the crest and onto the prairie, I wondered why a dead body seemed so much heavier than a living one.

I decided to rename the butte Otis Butte. Otis would lie forever under its grasses and weeds, or in the juniper tree, if his spirit made it there. It was his butte. I never knew the other people buried in the cemetery, and no one was left in the town to bury there, anyway.

I couldn't decide whether to unwrap Otis from the deerskin. Considerable work had gone into fashioning it—the hides of four animals and several nights' sewing with thread of tendons. To give it up now would mean creating another problem in the cool season, how to cover the cave entrance, that I might not be able to solve on my own. I was afraid to see Otis's face (what if it were bashed in?)

but at the same time wanted to, one last time, and if decay were a precondition for turning into a spirit, Otis might never decompose wrapped in layers of deer hide, bound with a yellow rope, and covered with dirt. He might never be able to find his wife.

That was it, then.

I untied the yellow rope and shook the deerskin as though I were airing out a blanket. As Otis rolled onto the trampled grass, I almost expected him to open his eyes and start breathing, but he was soft and motionless, his face undamaged from the battering descent.

I'm sorry that I no longer have the old photographs, from the time when Otis was young and strong and living with Malèna in Bismarck. Of course, those photographs wouldn't offer much of a clue to what he looked like when he died: an emaciated old man, with yellow-greenish skin tight over high cheek bones, a mouth open in a painful "O," teeth bared and crooked, a nose beaked like that of a hawk, and silver hair flowing to his shoulders so he seemed like a cross between an animal and a spirit. If I had had a camera, this is the photograph I would have made: Otis lying east to west at the foot of the juniper on Otis Butte above the White Earth River. No fancy clothes, no plates of food, and no wife to hold hands with. Just him alone in his tattered and dirty clothes.

Wrapping Otis in his sheet would have made the burial more dignified, but running back to the cave to fetch it would leave him unwatched under the lowering sky. I braided his hair instead and tied it with a section of yellow rope.

The bottom of the grave was dark, with roots crossing from one wall to the other that Otis would have to pass under. And then there was the dirt to shovel. I shuddered at the thought of throwing spadefuls of the rocky soil on his face. We didn't bathe often, but Otis was always fastidious about washing his face, and shaving the few hairs off his lip and chin with a knife, as though his face were sacred. This was something I never asked him about: Is the face sacred? I sat on the ground, my bowed legs dangling in the grave and held his cold forearm.

I pushed off and wrestled him down into the earth. His body became entangled in the roots, and I let go of him, throwing my hands against the damp soil to steady myself while I gagged and spit out the sour fluid that had come up from my stomach. I drew my knife and hacked at the roots. Otis's corpse dropped and landed with a thud on my feet. There were words that the ancestors, someone's ancestors, at least, used to chant to speed the deceased on to the next life, but I forgot to recite these. My throat burned. I straightened his twisted body and climbed out of the hole. I wiped my hands on my pants and brushed the dirt from my shoulders and chest as though I were shooing death away.

I grabbed the shovel and with a grunt rammed its blade into the pile of dirt. As I heaved the yellow-brown soil into the grave, I closed my eyes and listened to it fall on Otis's body and pretended I wasn't the one filling his grave.

I didn't stomp down the mound of dirt over his grave for fear of crushing his body. Rain and time would eventually settle the fine particles of soil and rocks. I stepped back, easing my weight onto the long handle of the shovel. The sharp dense leaves of the juniper bent in the wind. I thought of all the adversity we had suffered since the Event: food shortages, sickness, cold, heat, storms, bad water, bugs, boredom, and fear. Sometimes I was miserable, barely able to tolerate our life, but this moment was the worst. I let go of the shovel, and as it fell, I looked toward the dark, cloud-filled sky and cried:

Granddaddy, the earth's on top of you now!
But I still hear your voice and see your face.

I'm here, and you're somewhere else.

Is that what you meant by lives?

Tell me, what's a spirit?

I'm the only one left!

Why did you do this to me?

It wasn't what Otis had taught me to sing. It wasn't even a song, just random words that barely expressed the desperation I felt. Rain began to fall and dampen the raw earth of the grave. I told myself then that I would dig my own grave next to Otis's and wait for death at the bottom, with dirt piled along the four edges so the rain could wash it down over my body. I wanted Otis to be the first one to greet me in death.

I knocked dirt from the shovel and rolled up the deerskin. The bundle was tighter and narrower without Otis inside, and I wouldn't need to unroll it until the cool season. I left the yellow rope on the ground. I never wanted to see it again.

PART II:
WHITE EARTH RIVER (ALONE)

For the first days after I buried Otis, I didn't want to leave the cave. I spent mornings in bed as the dim light of dawn grew to the full sun of midday, when the sand on the ledge outside the cave became too hot for bare feet. Some days I stayed in the shade of the cave's opening, sitting in my chair, my elbows on my knees, and my head in my hands while I stared stupidly out at Otis Butte until the earth rolled into night. The time between dusk and sleep was cursed with the sounds of deer and pronghorn, their hooves striking the firm ground as they thundered down the butte to the valley meadows. But when I stepped outside the cave and peered over the ledge, I couldn't see them; perhaps I had heard only the spirits of these animals out on an evening prowl.

I called to them, as one animal would to another, in grunts, barks, hoots. I remembered the tune to the song I was supposed to chant for Otis's burial. But despite the months of practice, my mouth had forgotten how to form Otis's made-up Hidatsa words, and they came out as angry moans and groans, throaty monotone lines, broken up shouts and yells. I screamed in high pitches until my throat hurt and I exhausted myself. I danced in the sand outside the cave's entrance. As long as I was moving, loneliness couldn't settle on me and I could trick myself into believing that I was performing this ritual for Otis and that he could hear me.

Birds seemed to be the only ones who answered my singing—with a loud burst as they took off from their roosts in trees lining the butte's gullies and flew into the night. Perhaps my singing frightened them. Or maybe they thought the echo bouncing off Otis Butte was Otis's spirit answering me? The thought of this made me shout with greater fury. But I heard only my voice.

My voice didn't hold up. It became raw and sore. During the day, when I talked to myself, my words sounded like pebbles rattling in a rusty can. I began to think I was sick but couldn't bear the silence that came from not talking or singing. I brewed red root tea to soothe my throat. I began to hate living in the damp, heavy air of the cave, which still smelled of Otis. I packed a rucksack, not with much, just the essentials, and headed to the grove of cottonwoods and set up camp.

The route down the butte seemed steeper than usual and the distance to the valley greater than I had remembered. I barely recognized the garden as the one I had planted just a few weeks ago, perhaps because the weeds were as high as the plants. I felt alone and exposed in the openness of the valley, which had become foreign to me.

When my hunger finally spiked, I dropped to my hands and knees and grazed like a four-legged animal. I ripped dark-green leaves of spinach from their stalks and stuffed them in my mouth; snapped off asparagus stalks, tearing clean the tender tips with my teeth and chewing the fibrous stems into a pulp; pulled peas by the handful from their vines and crunched them to a mash; ate young onions and cloves of garlic until my mouth screamed.

I wished for a deer but knew that even a newborn fawn would require a brutal struggle and produce more venison than I could eat in a week. Instead of setting traps for small game, like rabbit, I let myself become distracted by a gopher that had tunneled under the black mesh netting meant to protect the garden from deer. Perhaps I thought he'd be easy to catch. His tracks led to a den in a corner of the cornfield. A light wire snare would surely catch him.

In the afternoon heat I sat in the grass and stared at the den's opening and sweated, believing my concentration would raise the animal from the ground. "Gopher, gopher resting below, you'll soon be dead, and roasting over a fire," I hummed, my song keeping me company. Shortly before dusk the animal waddled into the snare. As it struggled against the wire, I clubbed it with the blunt edge of the machete and then quickly dragged it away from its tunnel; other gophers might still be underground that I could later trap.

Its meat was greasy and gamey, not as delicate as rabbit or grouse, or deer killed quickly before fear spread through muscle and spoiled the taste. Cooking it hadn't been worth the trouble. I threw its small carcass into the fire and smelled the foul, lowly spirit of the animal. I added wood to make the fire burn hotter and rid the air of its putrid odor.

At night, under the trees, I wrapped myself in a deerskin, not just as a precaution against snakes and insects, but also to remember the sensation of Otis's tucking me in bed when I was a child. Beside a low fire I lay sweating, with the river of the Milky Way spread over me and the long night before me. I searched the sky for satellites—Otis had sworn they were up there, watching everyone, polluting the constellations—but all I could see were the familiar Big Dipper and an occasional dying star. Morning light could not arrive soon enough, and when it did, I shivered over a small fire and cup of tea, thankful for the strenuous labor and heat that the day would bring to distract me from my life.

I attacked the garden in a campaign to restore order. I crouched over the rows of plants and tore out weeds, in my haste leaving behind roots. My back ached from the hours spent leaning over, and my skin smarted from the sun, but I was grateful for the exhaustion and distraction that came from the labor. Otis's carefully thought out schedule of staggered planting had seemed so easy to follow when he was alive, but now remembering the scheme taxed my nervous mind and I had to run up to the cave in midday to consult old sketches of the plan to avoid making mistakes in the second phase of planting.

As the days passed, with a second then a third weeding, I began to see a fitness return to the garden. The rows of plants looked neat and tidy, almost happy. The leafy stalks of cottonwood saplings, driven into the ground and arching over the bedding plants, provided shade for the young growth until I thinned and transplanted the seedlings into full sun to mature. I staked the beans and reinforced the black mesh netting surrounding the garden, the same type of netting I used to trap deer, with lengths of straight green wood. With the bladders we had made from the mottled inner tubes in the boathouse, I hauled water from the river and irrigated the crops. I spread compost around the plants.

The days of hard work brought calmness, and I began to crave a reward, something sweet, for my effort. The honey in the beehives was ready, but Otis had always been the one to risk getting stung as we gathered the thick liquid and waxy combs. June berries were too green to release their nutty flavor. Chokecherries and wild plums weren't ripe.

An apple would have to do. I waded through grassy meadows to the road and walked north up the widening valley to the abandoned orchard. As the grass brushed against my legs, I remembered how I'd hold Otis's hand when I was young. For a moment, I didn't feel alone. He took me to the orchard only once a year, at the end of the warm season, declaring that in venturing so far we risked being detected. Of course, his lectures never stopped my running ahead and grabbing the low-hanging green and red fruit. He and I would fill the wheelbarrow and our packs with apples, dry some to cache for the cool season, and eat others over the course of several weeks, sometimes cooking them into a sweet, concentrated sauce. But that day, when I wanted a treat, the apples were barely fruit at all, just small, swollen balls on the stem, with none rotting on the ground to scavenge.

I shook a limb in anger. Of course I knew that fruit ripened once a season, but Otis had never talked about the apples' growing time, only his fear of encountering government agents. It was stupid of me not to have figured this out, one more thing that I didn't understand or couldn't remember.

I retraced my steps through the trampled grass, brushing up against the sharp spines of thistle, and passing dense rows of junipers that appeared in odd locations, as though they had once marked something that no longer existed, a roadway or path, perhaps. There were plenty of young milkweed buds to pick; at least these could add variety to my usual diet of corn, although they weren't sweet like an apple.

As I walked down the valley from the abandoned orchard, I saw the ruins of the town ahead, blurry in the midday heat. The cottonwoods and elms lining the road almost hid the demolished prefabs, and if I concentrated on the road, the river, the fields of grass along the floodplain, and the buttes framing the valley, I could pretend that someone at the end of the road would greet me and offer shelter.

Between the trees off to the right of the road, sunlight reflected off the metal roof of the monorail platform. Three idle silver cars rested on the track as though ready to take on passengers. A few times Otis and I had waited out afternoon storms under the protection of the metal roof as a torrent of hail drummed above. The machine operators who had knocked down the town had ignored the train cars and station—the concrete and steel would have required too much bashing and slamming to destroy, I suppose.

On the platform I peered through the window of the middle train car. Red seats brighter than any flower lined the walls, just below the windows, and tile the color of young sheaves of corn covered the floor. The door would not budge. Otis had never been very curious about the train. He worried that if we broke in, the town's power supply would magically switch on and we'd be whisked away to the Center for processing. I didn't share his fear. I wanted to sit on one of the red seats. I hoped the train car would take me somewhere.

I swung the ax at the door as though I were rescuing people trapped inside. I split the rubber gasket down the middle and smashed the mechanism that had kept the door locked for seventeen years. The door's two panels separated and rolled apart easily, with barely a nudge, as though they were welcoming me inside. The interior of the car smelled of heat and something else, perhaps the odor of the last passengers or the plastic of the red seats. I settled into their soft foam. The aluminum shell cracked with the exit of baked air, and sun shined through the windows. My head became heavy. I stretched out along the bench of seats, my nose pressed into the red foam, and inhaled the scent of the last person to sit there. Then I fell asleep.

I awoke chilled at twilight and returned to the garden. I picked a few leaves of lettuce and chewed a handful of sunflower seeds as the Big Dipper brightened, then collected my belongings and returned to the monorail car. On the green floor I spread the deerskin and cotton blanket; on the red seat I set my pack. Before lying down, I closed the door as though I were saying goodnight to my neighbors and shutting out the primitive world of spirits in which Otis roamed.

In the morning, light filled the car. Unlike in the cave, there were no corners of darkness. My shoulders and hips ached from the hard floor, so after tea I cut sod for a bed. It would dry quickly in the day's heat, as would the handfuls of grass I spread to add another layer of softness.

As I closed the door to my new dwelling to start the day's work in the garden, I said: "I live in a silver home above ground. It has windows and a door that opens and closes. I will never sleep in the earth again."

I became sick of the sound of my voice. The wordless singing, the monotonous humming, the jabbering to myself—a poor substitute for speaking to another person. I started to drum, instead.

With two cottonwood sticks the length of my forearm, I pounded on any hard surface available: the shiny side of the monorail car; the tree stump mortar in which I ground corn; the bench in the cottonwood grove; the plastic bucket in which I hauled foul-tasting water from the well; and the thick table under the pavilion where town residents, perhaps my parents, had once picnicked. This was my favorite spot because the pavilion's wooden roof and location on a rise trapped and amplified my singular drumming so it sounded as loud as a drum circle—what Otis had said was once a feature of the pow wows that he and Sammy had organized—and I imagined my father here, drumming beside me.

I was not silent as I pounded out a rhythm. The rapid beat of the sticks stretched my voice to new levels as I made up songs: shouts of descriptions of whatever activity I was about to do, was doing, or had done in the moments before, with the last syllable of a mournful moan held until my voice broke. I yelled, too, bringing up deep guttural sounds, as I had taught myself to do in the cave, until my throat hurt and my chest was coated in sweat.

One afternoon under the picnic pavilion, while drinking water from a leaky plastic bottle, I decided I would look for my parents. I would take a canoe and paddle downriver and out into the lake. I would sail up lake and down lake and scout the shore for other towns. If Otis and I had survived here in White Earth River, my parents may have survived in another town along a tributary or the lake itself, where there was arable land, fish to catch, animals to trap. Our survival proved that it was possible for other people to survive, too. Perhaps they had banded together with other overlooked people.

I beat the picnic table with my sticks, denting the wooden surface. When I finished, my hands sore from gripping the sticks, I looked across the river at the geese nesting on Goose Peninsula. They seemed not to have paid any attention to me. My music could not interrupt their eating and shitting.

"We could use them to fish." I had tried to sound practical the first time I had asked Otis about taking a canoe out on the river, but really I had wanted to know how it felt to float downstream like a branch. "What if we capsize? We'd drown," Otis had answered. "The boats will protect us," I had countered. Otis had laughed: "Just because you're on the surface doesn't mean you're safe."

Otis was afraid of the river because he had never learned to swim. I discovered this one evening when I waded too far into the channel of the river and slipped beneath the surface. Otis made no effort to rescue me and stayed in the ankle-deep water near shore.

That was my first swimming lesson: flailing my arms and kicking my feet to regain contact with the bottom. Later, I taught myself to dog paddle across the deep pools of the river; then I started to read one of the "Safe Boating" pamphlets I had found in a desk drawer in the boathouse.

The metal door to the boathouse rattled as I raised it. Sunlight washed over the mast, boom, rudder, and leeboards, which were spread over the floor where I had left them. I hadn't sailed the canoe since that day when I had showed Otis his grave. Outside the back door of the boathouse, on the ramp that angled down to the dock, a warm breeze rose off the White Earth River. Water lapped against the rotting boathouse pilings.

My favorite canoe, the sleek red one, was resting on a rack inside the boathouse. I wrestled it off the cradle and dragged it down the shaky ramp. I selected a life preserver and threaded my arms through the openings and buckled it, as the children in the "Safe Boating" pamphlet did. Three bulky rowboats filled with water were resting on the bottom of the river near the dock. Bailing one out would have taken all day, and they looked so fat and slow. I gathered up a paddle and the rigging.

The current led me south past Goose Peninsula and then around gentle bends until the river straightened and widened into the open water of White Earth Bay, where the wind picked up. For a moment I drifted, letting the wind push the canoe broadside while I secured the mast and stowed the paddle. I recalled the sequence of getting underway: drop the leeboards and rudder, tug on the halyard line and tie it to the cleat, push the boom aside. The triangle of white nylon filled with wind. I was headed out on what the "Safe Boating" booklet described as "a port tack with a close-hauled sail."

At least the direction of the wind and the angle of the canoe in relation to it seemed roughly to match one of the illustrations. There were other words in the booklet that had sounded odd to me at first, too—beating, running, tacking, coming about—but soon I learned their meaning.

After a few tacks, I was approaching the point of land where the bay met the lake, a short peninsula. If I were wandering or searching for others, this would be a place to rest, spend a night, and wait.

What I found surprised me: a small wooden structure at the head of a clearing dotted with iron circles, fire pits, some of which still had the remains of burnt wood. The structure's slats were falling off and its roof was sagging; it was unsafe to enter. A sign beside the crooked doorway said, "White Earth Store and Campground. Register here." The store's worn and faded sign indicated that the store had been abandoned long ago. I was sure all its food had been looted. Nonetheless, the remains of campfires and a gravel road leading away from the campground made me believe that people had stayed here. White Earth River seemed suddenly not to be so remote and isolated.

It didn't seem safe to explore up the gravel road. It would be better to watch the road from the lake, in case a group of people was traveling along the road. I wanted only to question one person at a time about my parents. That would be wisest. I pushed the canoe through the silt until it floated free.

With the buttes no longer breaking the wind's force, I could feel the thin plastic skin of the canoe straining against the water as the sail filled and tightened. I leaned against the gunwale to balance the boat and pressed the tiller toward the water. This was the first time I had sailed beyond the mouth of the bay. I tried to stay near the shore to keep an eye on the road leading to the campground, but after a few hundred meters, an inlet appeared: a marsh of thick reeds waded into the water, fields of grasses and flowers dropped off to a border of driftwood and rocks and silt, and narrow stands of alluvial trees marched up the side of a butte. The land looked continuous and wild, as though it had always been that way and I was the first to see it. There was no sign of the road or another town.

The wind carried me into the middle of the lake. I was afraid to fight it, to try to come about and steer the boat back to shore. Soon I was as far from one shore as another, both blurry in the distance. I felt locked in the water, the sail tight. Moments passed—how many I'm not sure. I hung onto the tiller. The risk of swamping and capsizing edged into my mind, and I tried not to think about how quickly I had left the shore behind.

My mind began to empty out. Water rushed along the sides of the canoe and sprayed my hands, my face. I started to enjoy the tension between water and wind and sail. It was as though I weren't alone. Then I glanced over my shoulder, curious about how far I had come. This was a mistake: it broke the trance. The shore was a haze; I couldn't see the entrance to the bay; and fear of not returning spilled over me. In a panic I pulled in the sail to come about. The sail flapped violently, the mainsheet dug into my hand, and chop hit the stalled canoe. Sour fluid rose into my mouth. I spit into the lake and pushed aside the boom, let out the sail, and ran toward shore.

I dropped the sail and drifted. The air had chilled me, my fingers were numb from clutching the mainsheet, and the muscles in my arms, the first time they had been tensed in this way, shook. I held onto the gunwales for balance and tried to understand what I had experienced. Something in the lake, in the movement of the canoe through the water, had spoken to me, but I didn't know what this force was trying to say to me. I wondered if I was on the verge of having a vision.

After that day, I sailed down lake every afternoon. At first I looked for towns. When I didn't find any, I searched for the feeling I had experienced on the first day. It eluded me. I returned to the dock exhausted and burned from the sun and wind and craving food and water. I tried to remember the connection between water, wind, and sail. When these elements had lined up, it was like the first bite of deer meat. Not sweet or sour or bitter or hot, but of the deer, what the deer was willing to give up, leave behind.

PART III: THE STRANGER

I heard the sound as I approached the peninsula. It had a quality unlike any of the sounds I had become dependent on for company: wind rattling the sail, water rushing along the hull of the canoe, the snap of rigging against the mast. It was a human sound, a faint singing, and seemed to be coming from the road and drifting over the silt flats and cottonwood saplings and across the water toward me.

The closer I got to shore, the louder and more regular the singing became, with a stop and start rhythm to a peculiar melody. I dropped the sail and drifted and strained to hear the tune: lines slightly echoing, rhyming, and rising like a question. I bobbed my head as a voice sang:

> I don't know but I've been told
> Working in a quarry gets mighty old.
> I don't know but it's been said
> Bust your ass and end up dead.
>
> Cruising along and making time
> Wind at my back and feeling fine.

Tire blew out and lost control
Hit the brakes but started to roll.

Cut and scraped and bleeding, too,
But sucked it up and tied my shoe.
Started to walk and felt the pain
Cried for Momma and prayed for rain.

No one here in this goddamn place
Looks to me like the end of the race.
Stomach churning, starting to yell
Soon I'll die and rot in hell.

The words were English, the song unlike anything Otis had ever sung. I looked toward the clearing above the silt flats and saw a huge man standing in the middle of the campground. I froze in place, both hands on the gunwales to steady myself. An agent, surely. But he wasn't wearing the gray suit that Otis had told me that agents wear. Nor was he carrying a gun. And he continued to sing as he walked in a circle around the campground. A government man wouldn't sing to himself as he carried out the work of rounding up or killing people, I thought. Nor would he walk around in shorts and no shirt, showing off his hairy chest. Even before the town emptied out and was destroyed, we didn't have many neighbors; a few farms, maybe some distant towns—ours was not a populous region, Otis used to say. Perhaps he was from one of those places, left behind and now coming out from hiding. Perhaps he had encountered my parents.

The stranger dropped his small pack and walked onto the silt flats, where he kneeled and washed his face and drank several handfuls of the chalky water—not a good health practice, and proof that he wasn't from an abandoned farm. A farmer would know better.

When he stood up, he brought his hands level to his forehead as though to scout the lake. I wasn't far offshore; I'm sure the stranger must've seen me immediately. Yet, at first he didn't react. Perhaps he wasn't expecting to see another person, and I felt unsure about whether I wanted to be seen.

"Hey!" the stranger shouted. "You!"

This voice was louder than the one he used to sing and had a shrill ring to it.

"Hey, you, I need some help!"

I didn't believe him. He didn't seem to be hurt, and his size was threatening. Perhaps he was trying to fool me, lure me ashore for an attack. Despite the danger, I wanted to see what this giant of a man looked like up close. I lowered the sail and paddled slowly toward shore, careful not to run aground in the thick silt of the shallows. I drew figure eights with the paddle to keep the canoe from washing onto shore with the wind.

The stranger began lifting one leg at a time as he moved through ankle-deep water toward me in an odd, belabored dance. Suddenly he started shouting:

"Hydraulic mud! Sucking my shoes off my feet! You gotta help me, com! I'm misfiring!"

He sounded like he was going to cry. But I didn't believe this. I thought he was acting, the way Otis would when he spoke the different voices in *The Tale of the Prince Who Was Denied*. The silt would swallow my sandals, too, if they weren't tied on tight.

"You have to dig for them," I shouted across the water.

"What? My parents?"

"Only if they live at the bottom of the lake. Your shoes, I mean," I laughed.

The stranger squatted and plunged his hands into the silt, up to his elbows. "Might as well have my hand up my ass," he said more to himself than to me. He used words that I had never heard before, a secret language of sorts. One by one, he extracted his sneakers. He poured watery silt out of them, rinsed them, and then flung them on the shore. He advanced toward me, swaying from foot to foot, his hands out to his sides for balance, as though he were afraid to step on the muddy bottom. He would capsize the canoe; that would be next, I thought. Then we would be in the water together, fighting. His size and strength would allow him to push me to the bottom and hold me there until I drowned.

"You got any food?" he asked.

"Not here," I said, gripping the paddle so I could escape or hit him, if he lunged at me.

"What about at home?"

He wiped sweat from his burnt brow and took another step forward.

"No food there, either," I said.

"Come on, what d'you eat? I haven't had anything in three days!"

He took another step, and then I saw his face. I had never seen pictures of a person, man or woman, so hideous and couldn't stop myself from staring at the stranger's pink, sunburned flesh, his scraggly beard, peeling nose, and the lumpy white pustules disfiguring his skin. Curiosity made me want to paddle closer, but I didn't. He was already near enough that with a few quick strides he would be at my side. I back-paddled away from him.

"You have to catch it!" I shouted over the sound of my paddle sloshing water.

"What, com?! What am I going to catch?!" the stranger screamed, even though we were close enough to hear each other easily.

He was pushing through water toward me. Water was up to his thighs. Another step would bring it up to his hips, then he'd have to swim. That would be to my advantage: a canoe is faster than a swimmer. And I could always strike him in the hands or head as I paddled.

"I just used up my last bit of strength getting here! And that store is empty!"

His voice had degenerated into a high-pitched whine, a tone as ugly as his face.

Suddenly, he was thrashing, struggling to find footing. He must've stepped into a hole. He burst up from the water and gasped for air.

"Hydraulic son of a bitch! You want to kill me?" he screamed. "I don't know how to swim!"

I should have paddled away at that point and been done with him, but I enjoyed watching his torment. I'm not sure why. Perhaps because his size and ugliness, the coarse way he moved, and his high-pitched voice and odd words made him seem to be a different species from Otis and me. His lack of cleverness meant that I could always outsmart him and get away, if I needed to. So I continued to watch him.

The stranger seemed to give up. He staggered back to shore and picked up his shoes and began throwing them into the mud, first one, then the other, retrieved them and then threw them down again, uttering as they smacked the wet silt: "Mother shit. Father shit. Goddamn family shit." Then he laced them up and squished up the flats toward the campground and the empty, collapsing store.

I began to laugh at his confusion. He was lost, wandering from somewhere to someplace else, alone as he cursed his mother and father.

The stranger reminded me of my own hunger, and this stopped me from sweeping the paddle through the water and turning away from shore. My diet of fish and vegetables hadn't been very filling, or satisfying, and I was growing tired of the measly walleye I had been catching. After the poor experience with the gopher, I hadn't set any snares and had been too impatient to attempt netting a goose. The size of the stranger would be an advantage in capturing one, if I could lure him back to the playing field. And perhaps he'd passed other towns with people in them, places where I could search for my parents.

Of course, I didn't let the stranger enter the canoe; I kept him a safe distance from me.

"Hey!" I yelled. "We could catch a goose!"

The stranger turned.

"What?" he said.

"We could catch a goose. Cook it."

"What's a goose?"

"A big bird. Like a duck."

"Like a chicken? Like on National Tranquility Day?"

Otis had never told me about National Tranquility Day, but I didn't want the stranger to know this.

"Yeah, like a chicken," I said.

"Okay," the stranger said and walked down the silt flat toward me.

"We have to go up the bay and the river a little ways to where the geese live. It's not far. You can walk. There's no room in the canoe." I pointed to the sail and mast, stored in the front of the boat.

"I wouldn't get in that shaky thing even if there was room."

The stranger walked on the firm silt, well above the waterline, and could easily match the speed of the canoe. In fact, I found I had to paddle fast to keep up with him. I tried not to show that this was an effort and hoped he couldn't hear my rapid breathing.

Once we reached the river and started upstream, the stranger crossed the silt beaches and grassy banks without complaining. The distance didn't seem to tire him. Perhaps the promise of a goose calmed him. We didn't speak.

Before I had started my forays downriver, I had thought that our town was a long way from Lake Sakakawea. It wasn't, actually. It was situated along the wider, deeper section of White Earth River just a few long bends from the bay.

When we arrived at the playing field, I tied the canoe to the dock and stayed there, still preserving a distance between the stranger and me in case I needed to escape.

"Where're the geese, com?" the stranger asked.

"There," I pointed, "up in the playing field, in the grass. Listen," I said.

You could hear them moving about, pecking at the ground for seeds, insects, grass.

"Okay, traction. But how do we catch them?"

"You have to tackle them. I'll flush them toward you, you grab the fattest one you see."

"They're much bigger than the chickens we eat. More like little kids."

"Yeah, that's right. Like children. I catch them all the time."

"By yourself?"

"I used to do it with my grandfather."

"Traction."

I didn't offer the stranger use of the net with the sinkers tied along the edges, which is what I used to net a goose. I wanted to test his skill at hunting. If I were going to attempt trapping a deer with him, I wanted to be sure it wouldn't be a waste of energy, which would leave two hungry people to feed with only the vegetables from the garden.

As it turned out, the stranger didn't wait for me to herd the geese toward him; he set off alone in a sprint across the field, his arms wide, his body low to the ground. His attempts were so funny that laughter prevented me from leaving the dock. I was doubled over. His antics were better than any tale Otis had acted out.

He quickly came to appreciate that his best chance lay in separating a goose from the flock, but his timing was off. Whenever he dove toward the bird, it easily eluded him with a quick burst of flapping and its own sprint into taller grass. The stranger would hit the ground with a "thump" before rising up to swear in a way I'd never heard before: "Hydraulic son of a bitch!"

I didn't think he'd be able to catch one, and his show of diving into the grass made me not care. Why was this so funny? I don't know. Perhaps it reminded me of playing soccer with Otis, chasing the ball, kicking it, his bouncing it off his head, our shouts and laughter, one of the few times it seemed that there were more people than just Otis and me in White Earth River.

But suddenly the game ended. The stranger caught a goose, a lone, midsize one, a year or two old. He was hugging it against his chest, trying to subdue it. One wing dangled limply, misshapen, perhaps broken from the struggle. It was still alive, and angry. Its long neck twisted and turned wildly so it could peck the stranger's arms and face. I ran as fast as I could. I knew he wouldn't be able to hold it for very long.

The stranger was leaning backward, turning his head away from the goose, which had began to squawk. The stranger seemed to be squeezing it tighter and tighter in an attempt to kill it.

I grabbed the goose's neck with both hands and gave it a sharp snap and then pulled the bird to the ground and severed its neck with my knife. The stranger jumped back as blood oozed from the stump.

"Oh, you little ragamuffin bastard! You just cut its fucking head off! Brutal, com, brutal!"

He shook his hands as though he had slaughtered the goose and was ridding them of blood.

I held the bird until it was still.

"You have to kill him right away, not let him suffer."

"I don't know about killing a geese."

"Goose."

I looked up at the stranger. His eyes were light brown, greenish, not black like Otis's or mine. A blank expression hung on his bumpy face, which was now covered in welts. His slack jaw blended into his neck. Although he was tall, he wasn't old, perhaps only a little older than I was.

The smell of blood, intestines, and flesh as I cut the goose open made my stomach rumble with hunger. I imagined the taste of the meat, hot and oily and gamey.

"Gather some wood," I ordered. I scooped heart, lung, and bowels from the bird's cavity and then wiped my hands on the grass.

"What's that, gather wood?"

"From the trees, twigs and branches, the dry ones. Pick them off the ground."

The stranger looked at me dumbly.

"All right, follow me," I said.

I was afraid to leave the goose, in case a coyote or fisher was watching, so I carried it. The feathers still needed to be plucked.

"That thing is still bleeding," the stranger said.

"It'll stop," I said.

"I mean, I was just walking down the road, you know, looking for something to eat."

"Me, too."

"Then we're on the same team, right?"

"We're not playing soccer."

"What's that?"

"A game. Teams play it."

"Like Hug the Tree?"

"What's Hug the Tree?"

"Fathers and sons play it after dinner, in the woods, when everyone's drunk. If you catch a father, you get to beat him. If a father catches you, he gets to beat you. Hug the Tree."

"Soccer's not like that. You play it with a ball. You kick it and try to score goals."

Otis and I had played soccer until the ball went flat. He had never talked about the sports that people on the preserves or in the Center played, because he didn't know about them, but it didn't surprise me that the stranger would play the type of game he described. He'd probably been caught many times by the fathers and most of the beatings he'd suffered had probably been to his head.

A round rod of metal fit into a slot in my knife sheath, and if I struck the rough metal at the right angle, it generated a spark. This I did, squatting over the fire ring. A pile of dry grass began to smoke. I lowered my face toward the grass and blew long and steady. The grass glowed, and the kindling caught and crackled.

"Voom, then there's fire!" the stranger said. "I've never seen anything like this. First it's the bird, now this. You look like you do it all the time, com."

"Pretty often," I said, rising up.

The stranger kneeled down beside the fire ring. "We have a stove at home. Electric. We use it to boil water for packages."

Packages. We had found a few of those in the ruins. I plucked the goose. The feathers and down would add another layer to the pillow I had started before Otis had died.

"This place is kind of run down, you know," the stranger said, looking around. "That table over there? It's missing some boards, and all the shit."

I ignored the nervous way he spoke and thought about how the goose wasn't large, not a mature adult, the ones I preferred to cull from the flock, and that I deserved a larger portion because I had killed and cooked it.

"I've seen 'em fly overhead before, honking. Your parents know you kill 'em?" the stranger asked.

"They don't know what I do," I said, which, of course, was true.

"Yeah, mine don't either. Not any more. After I grabbed a bunch of MRGs and jumped on my bike."

"You rode to the lake?" I looked at his face.

"Yeah. Almost." He smiled. "I was fed up with the quarry. Just pedaled away. No one came after me."

"Where's your bike?" I asked. Otis had hoped to find one in the ruins but never did.

"Busted. In a ditch somewhere. I crashed."

The stranger began rocking back and forth on his heels. His knee was swollen. The skin around a large scab was red, probably infected.

"Oh. Did you meet anyone on the road named Pérez?"

"Pérez? No. No Pérezes. Nobody at all. Everything's deserted. Why?"

"That's my father."

"He doesn't live here?"

"No, just me."

"Alone?"

"My grandfather used to be here, but he died."

"Then you're alone."

"Yeah."

"You're alone. I'm alone. We're the same."

"A little, maybe."

I skinned four willow branches on which to skewer the goose.

"Then we don't have to share the bird with your parents or your grandfather."

"No."

"You really know how to use that thing." He pointed to my knife. "Where'd you get it?"

"My grandfather."

"I had grandparents, too. They died a long time ago, I think. My dad said that they weren't useful. My mom won't talk about it."

"Were they relocated or killed?" I asked.

"I don't know. Killed, probably," the stranger said.

"That's what usually happens."

"Yeah."

I stirred the coals and lowered the rusty grill, spacing the halves of the goose equally over the heat. I brushed some goose scat out of the way and sat in the grass with my legs to the side. The stranger rocked off his knees to sit beside me.

"How's my face look, is it really bad?" He touched the goose welts, the white-tipped bumps, his scraped nose, and the beginnings of a beard.

"Pretty bad," I told him.

"Damn, that bird. My bike crash, too. And I haven't shaved since I left."

"You smell like the geese."

"Their shit. I know. It's on my shoes."

"On your shirt, too."

I felt the stranger study me and looked straight ahead, toward the fire, to avoid his stare.

"And *your* shorts are kind of dirty. And torn up, too," he pointed at me.

I had found the pants in a demolished closet, not on a skeleton, and had cut off the legs below the knee. They hung loosely, held up with the deer hide belt on which I carried my knife.

"They're okay," I said.

"And those shoes. I've never seen any like them."

"My grandfather made them." I wanted to recount how the garden cart tire had gone flat, how we had tanned the hide but stopped myself, afraid of revealing too much about my life.

"He must've been clever. My uncle's clever. He lives in the Center. He said he'd get me a job there. At the cathedral, maybe."

"That's a type of preserve?" I ventured. Otis had told me about the office towers he'd helped build but was ignorant of the final form the Center had taken. I moved the pieces of goose so the flames from the fat didn't singe the skin too much.

"Some kind of monument. Like a park. People visit it for fun. To sit inside and be quiet. Its walls need tons of pink granite. What we mined in the quarry. I'm a mason. Finishing team. Want to see my tools?"

The stranger pulled two hammers from his pack. One had a pick on its end and the other had a wide, flat blade. A bright loop of red cord ran through their yellow plastic handles.

I gently swung the one with the pick. It was well balanced, of good workmanship. I imagined the damage the pick could do: pierce a hand, lodge between a rib, split open a skull. It would have been easy for me to turn on him and wound him, maybe kill him, with one strike, or for him to do the same to me. But we were getting along; we were sharing a goose; he seemed okay, if odd. I handed him the tools, unafraid that he'd suddenly attack me, and he began rhythmically planting them in the grass. I almost asked if he wanted to whittle with my knife.

"When I get to the Center, I'll have to sneak in, probably at night. Then I'll find my uncle," he said.

"You'll be detected."

"There might be a small problem. Usually, transfers are arranged beforehand, true, but my uncle can probably smooth things out. You could come with me. Look for that guy, Perrr . . ."

"Pérez."

"Yeah, Pérez."

"My father."

"Yeah, your father. He might be in the Center."

"I don't know. I don't like agents."

"Yeah, I don't either. But if your father's there, it won't matter."

I checked the temperature of the goose by sticking the point of my knife into its flesh. The spurt of juice made my mouth water. It was done. I handed the stranger the skewers with the smaller half of the goose.

"I wish my mom could see me now." A chirp, an aborted laugh, gurgled up through his throat. "Eating a bird and it's not even National Tranquility Day. You have a knife and fork? I know how to use them."

"No," I lied, even though we had several in the cave.

I crunched the small bones of the breast and sucked the marrow out of the thigh and waited for the stranger to notice that he had less food than I did. He seemed not to understand that he had been cheated and left ample meat on the bones, which I asked to eat.

"Yeah, if you want. I don't eat the bones, and this bird didn't taste that good. Kind of tough and stringy. But I'm still hungry. I could eat another, I guess. If you'll cook it, I'll catch it."

"Not so soon, they're still upset."

"Then you have something else to eat?"

"We could fish later." I wasn't about to mention the garden.

"What about some MRGs?"

MRGs, what was he talking about?

"No, there aren't any" seemed a safe response.

I placed the fat-coated sticks on the fire so they would flare up.

"Well, I guess I can wait until dinner. The clinic says I need about 5,000 calories a day. And I'm depleted. I don't need a test to tell me that."

The stranger sighed, pried off his sneakers, and then lay on his back, stretching to his full length. He wiggled his toes, flexed his ankles, and laced his fingers beneath his head as though he were going to take a nap.

Although we were getting along, seeing him relax infuriated me. Did he think he could stay in White Earth River without my asking him to? That I would feed him and offer him shelter on my land? What right did he have even to be here? I looked at his bright, shiny red shorts and white T-shirt with the number seven on the front, stained from sweat and grass and smeared with goose shit. I smelled his rotten odor, worse than the smell of shit. I imagined him a huge, oddly proportioned carcass, dead on the ground, ready to be gutted.

I stirred the coals so the fire would burn itself out and then stood up. "I need to go. I have work to do."

"Wait, I'll help you. I'm a good worker, strong as a machine."

The stranger sat up and shoved his blistered feet into his shoes.

"I have to do it by myself."

"Why? You got a solitary?"

"Yeah."

The stranger seemed to talk about things that even Otis hadn't known existed.

"But what about later, com?" His voice tightened and rose in pitch again, in the wounded tone he had spoken in before.

"Aren't you going to the Center?" I asked.

"I need to build up my stores, com. I'm nearly finished. And that fucking bird was just a snack."

His eyes were like those of a frightened animal, half-dead in a snare. I didn't want to be near him. I'd never trap a deer with him, despite his strength. I shouldn't have fed him, delayed his death.

"Maybe I'll see you later," I said and then jogged off into the woods to avoid his catching up with me before I crossed the river and disappeared into the ruins of the town.

I stopped in the garden and at the monorail car to stuff my pack with vegetables and gather the deerskin and bladders of water. As I climbed up Windy Butte, the space the stranger filled in my mind seemed to expand and bump up against the spaces that had contained my life up to this point: Otis's confession; my parents' disappearance; my life alone in the cave, garden, and monorail car; my sailing and drumming and search. There didn't seem to be enough room in my head for everything. The borders stretched and then broke because the area the stranger occupied, like the stranger himself, was larger than everything else.

Outside the cave, alertness, more acute than any I had experienced before, warned me not to step inside the cave. It would have been impossible for the stranger to know its location and to have raced up the butte before me to hide in it, but this is what I feared. I settled onto the sandy ledge outside the cave, my back pressed against the warm sandstone of the butte, and watched over the valley.

What was the stranger doing? Where would he sleep? Was he still hungry? Why did I care? We had shared a meal, that was all, but now I found myself able only to think about him, his bulky size, his high-pitched voice, ugly face, and funny way of talking. Why did I lead him to White Earth River? Otis would never have done this, even to help with trapping game. And, yes, Otis would be mad at me right now. I imagined the stranger becoming tried of waiting for me to return and leaving. Or, if it were true that he hadn't eaten in three days, maybe he'd wander the empty ruins of the town, unaware of the garden, until he fell down in a thistle-choked street and died.

At dusk I unrolled the deerskin on the sandy ledge outside the cave. The crude map in my mind continued to shift to accommodate this disturbing person. I pulled the drumming sticks from my belt and threw them into the cave. This was not a time to think about singing.

Sometime during the night I crawled under the deerskin and stayed there until the sun was midway toward overhead and the sky was a bright, cloudless blue. The intensity of the heat and the light tormented me. A crust of sand covered my lips, and grit had filled my mouth. The wind had forced grains of sand into every crevice of my body: the split of my buttocks, the moist fold of my groin, the corners of my eyes, the creases alongside my nose. Not even my foreskin escaped the sand, which I discovered when I walked to the far corner of the ledge and pissed an amber stream that burned my penis. Dehydration. The stranger's presence had upset my routines for eating and drinking and now I was suffering. He had been right, though: half a goose wasn't much to eat. Otis and I would've shared a pot of corn mush, too, and a few stalks of broccoli.

I washed the sand from my face and mouth with handfuls of water. I craved a hot cup of red root tea but was afraid to light a fire, in case the smoke gave away my location. Instead, I sipped water and slowly chewed leaves of curly kale, which was not my favorite kale.

Below me, in the tops of the cottonwoods, birds sang as though nothing were different in the valley: no starving man wandering the streets or waiting to rob me of what little food I carried in my pockets; no bloated corpse lying face down and beginning to rot.

This last thought preoccupied me, and although the stranger was still probably several days away from starvation, I couldn't rid my mind of an image of him face down on the ground, arms outstretched, and skin tight over his ribs—like the carcass of a pronghorn at the bottom of a cliff, swollen with gas and beginning to decompose.

I remembered my disgust in seeing flies crawl over Otis's cool, yellow-green face, the stench of his soiled clothing. I wouldn't bury another body. This time would be different. I'd hack the stranger's bloated corpse into pieces small enough for coyotes to carry away. Let them gnaw on the bones, shred the muscle, tendons, and vessels. Let the earth absorb his blood until all that remained of him was a stain on the ground.

As I rolled up the deerskin, the stranger's voice started to play a song in my head, not his words, or the catchy melody he had sung when I found him on the shore, but his tones and inflections, his bellowing and hearty *braa's*, *gaa's*, *coo's*, *whaa's*, and his whiny *aie's*, *eee's*, *iii's*. These ricocheted around in my head, bouncing off one side and zapping through to the other. These sounds were worse than the moaning that replayed itself in my head after I'd endured Otis's attempts at singing his fake Hidatsa songs.

I wanted to scream, long and loud, but was afraid of revealing my location. To rid my head of the stupid noise the stranger's speech had created, to clear up the confusion I was beginning to feel about whether he would starve or leave, I had to see him and hear his voice—and mine in response to his.

I would bring him clean water and vegetables. We would share another meal. I was ravenous.

Even though the rubber bladders made the well water taste fouler than it already was, I filled two of these and arranged a handful of young carrots and small zucchinis in the bottom of my pack. From the food cache in the garden, I stuffed my pockets with last season's sunflower seeds. I expected to find the stranger lying on a picnic table in the pavilion, but he wasn't there. Nor was he wandering through the ruins of the town, walking south or north along the road, or standing under the metal roof of the monorail platform, where I finally rested in the shade. Water had sloshed down my chest, and the rope joining the two bladders had dug into my neck. I was hot and irritable, sorry that I had gone to so much trouble for someone whose presence I resented. Maybe he had gotten tired of waiting for me to show up and left town. Or maybe he suddenly died, I thought. I readjusted the bladders and walked back toward the playing field. *Gaa, braa, whaa!*

Both doors of the boathouse were now raised, and the stranger was standing on the dock, facing upriver, his shorts down around his thighs. His pelvis was thrust forward as he aimed his long penis so an arc of urine fell into the river.

"There you are, you little ragamuffin son of a bitch!" He pulled up his shorts and bounded up the ramp to the boathouse and slapped me on the shoulder. "I was losing traction last night when you didn't show up. I thought I'd never see you again. Those blue things. Better than a broken table." He pointed at the bed of life preservers he had made on the floor.

Usually, the blue vests hung from the rack along the wall, lined up from small to large, with their zippers closed and buckles fastened, and it bothered me that he had rearranged them as if the boathouse were his. I slung the bladders over a peg in the wall and walked out onto the dock to see if the stranger's urine had changed the color of the water. He watched me from the boathouse, his arms crossed and chest puffed out.

"It's not good to piss in the river," I said, looking back at him, standing above me. "We bathe in it, and the fish live there. I'll show you the pit I squat over in the rubble later on."

I paused a moment and then recited a lecture that Otis had given me when we were bathing in the river: "The water isn't safe to drink. It's okay to wash in because our skin protects us, but never drink it." I could feel Otis's patient but stern voice overtaking my own as I spoke. I wasn't sure if what Otis believed was true. His fear of the water may have had more to do with his not knowing how to swim.

"Tasted okay to me." The stranger pouted and put his hands on his hips. "I've been drinking it all along." He had stopped smiling. "Ever since I started down the road to your dead-end shit part of the world."

"The river looks okay, but it's filled with chemicals from farming long ago. They'll make you sick." I continued Otis's argument.

The stranger walked the few steps down the ramp and onto the dock and peered into the water, then he stared at me. His eyes seemed darker than they had the day before.

"Why are you stalling out on me, com?" He whined and pointed a finger at me. "I thought we were going to have some fun today but you show up hitting me with don'ts."

He was taller than me by two heads, and while I was thinking about what to say, he closed in on me, pushing his weight forward and clenching his fists.

"No, this, out here"—I backed up and swept my hand through the air, indicating the river, destroyed town, and Windy Butte—"if you follow certain rules, you can live a long time." I couldn't stop myself from stating Otis's beliefs, but I knew I wasn't speaking with his authority.

The stranger smiled and leaned toward me. "Don't worry, little com, I'm just passing through," he boasted. "I don't plan on staying here long enough to die. Now what'd you bring me to eat?"

I took a step away from him and took the zucchinis and carrots from my pack.

The stranger bit off the tip of a carrot. "This one tastes like candy." He twisted off the green feathery leaves and dropped them on the dock.

"It's carrot. First of the season." I picked up the leaves. "Don't you want to eat the tops? That's where all the vitamins are."

The stranger tried them, but grimaced. "Not sweet at all, com. You can have them."

He ate three more carrots while I ate the leaves.

"Carrot, huh. Never heard of it, com. And what's this green one called?"

"Zucchini."

The stranger bit off the end and began chewing it.

"Firm, but not as good as carrot."

He sipped some water from a rubber bladder and wiped his mouth with the back of his hand.

"Better than the packaged stuff we usually eat, though," he said.

"All of our food comes from the garden," I said. "And gardens require work."

"Traction, com."

He didn't seem to care.

"So what else do you have for me?" he asked.

I decided not to share the sunflower seeds. There weren't many left in the cache, and the new crop wouldn't be ready to harvest until later in the warm season.

"Do you know how to fish?" I asked instead.

I thought fishing would test his capacity for patience and silence, two qualities essential for trapping a deer, something we could attempt in the afternoon, if the fishing went okay. It didn't. His casts were clumsy, and he swore when his rod hit the ground. Despite his outbursts, I caught three walleye, which I cooked in the coals of a fire. With my knife I removed the sweet flesh of the walleye from its skin and passed chunks to the stranger, who sat on a driftwood log while I squatted beside the fire. He tried not to let the oily meat slip off his fingers, but a few times it did. He picked it from the sand and ate without chewing, swallowing pieces whole, sand and all, and licked his fingers and lips after every bite. I sucked portions of the fish off the blade of my knife.

We didn't speak as we ate. Both of us were hungry, and I worried that, like the goose, the three fish wouldn't be enough. The stranger seemed to enjoy the taste of the walleye; at least he didn't complain. And perhaps because there were three of them and I was parceling out the meat, it seemed like more food than the skewers of goose had offered.

As we ate I reassessed his worth to me. So far he hadn't shown much aptitude for trapping and fishing. Of course, his size and strength would be a benefit in hauling water; his skill with mason's tools, in splitting wood. But could I teach him to pick vegetables without his destroying the plant? I doubted it. Perhaps he could learn to harvest geese with the net. What we really needed, though, was a deer. If he couldn't be quiet enough to lie in wait to net and wrestle one to the ground, perhaps he could run one to death. Or spear one. Otis and I had tried this, but after the first thrust (with knife tied to a stick), the deer had fled and we lost its track up the valley.

I weighed the benefit between feeding him long enough so he could contribute to food production and urging him to leave White Earth River right away. The more I thought about him, the more I worried that his flight from the quarry might bring agents to White Earth River. Perhaps he lied about having an uncle in the Center and

I would be stuck listening to the sound of his voice as I taught him skills for survival. And where would he live? Not in the cave, not in the monorail car. Perhaps he could live in the boathouse. Or perhaps he didn't want to stay. Perhaps after the meal of walleye, he'd have enough energy to leave.

As a start to fortifying him, for either trapping a deer or leaving (I still hadn't decided which I preferred), I gave him the entire third walleye. While he picked it apart, I stripped out of my shorts and waded into the river. The muddy bottom dropped off gradually, and the water cooled my body and eased the tension that had built up from my worry about the stranger. Seeing him in person, despite the irritations that came from being with him, had at least cleared the sounds of his speech from my head. I wondered if all people were like the stranger, so different from me, from Otis, and this is what you have to put up with to be with another person. Companionship didn't seem like it was worth all the trouble. Perhaps it would be different with my parents.

I washed the coating of dust from my body and then swam to a deep pool and dove to the rocky bottom. Fish scattered—another meal's worth, at least—and I dug my fingers into the bottom and floated, suspended, and let the cool water numb me, until I couldn't hold my breath any longer.

As I walked up from the river, I slicked back my black hair and squeezed water from the ends. I was small compared to the stranger. I lacked the thick, curly chest hair that made his muscles seem heavy and powerful. Except for a small patch around my penis, my body was nearly devoid of hair, most of it fine, barely visible, and the hair on my head was long and straight, not like the woolly thicket the stranger had. I felt him watching me. His hands were under his head, bending his neck forward so he could observe me. After a moment, he sat up and pointed at my legs.

"What's wrong with them, com?"

They had no bites, cuts, or rashes on them, so I knew he was referring to their shape.

"Nothing, they're fine," I said, not meeting his stare.

"Then why are they all bent out?"

I had once compared my legs to Otis's while we were bathing in the shallows. "Lack of food," Otis had told me. I had stopped breast-feeding a few months after I was born, the night my mother disappeared. I had only survived because Otis had chewed food and forced it into my mouth with his tongue. Still, it had taken me a long time to thrive. "Most weeks, I was ready to begin digging your grave," Otis had once recounted.

"They work fine." I stretched to my full height and faced the stranger.

"Traction, com, but they look funny. I'm surprised they let your parents keep you."

"Not everyone looks the same," I said.

My face grew warm, and I looked away.

"Ah, com, you're spraying me, now. I mean, what type of woman would want you with those legs? Certainly not one in the Center. They're all perfect. That's why I'm going there. To find a perfect one."

I wiped the grit from my feet and strapped on my sandals.

"I thought you were going to find your uncle," I said.

"That, too." The stranger shifted in the sand. "What do you think they look like?"

"What?"

"The women."

I thought about the book of photographs of Otis and Malèna in Bismarck.

"They have long black hair and wear special dresses and shoes that make them stand tall on their toes . . . and they like to sit at tables and eat big meals."

The stranger squirmed and leaned forward. He spread his legs wide, as though his testicles were large and needed extra space to rest in the sand.

"Right. They're all Office, School, or Clinic. They don't really work," he said.

He closed his eyes and opened his mouth, moving his jaw back and forth while he worked his hand into his shorts.

"Damn, this is going to be great. Center women are the best. That's what my uncle says. Firm, tight, beautiful."

He was grasping his penis now and had pushed down his shorts.

"Tell me, com, their tits, what do you think they're like?"

I imagined my mother, perhaps in a bed, perhaps in a folding chair, as she cradled me in her arms, my lips at her breast.

"Their breasts are full of milk so they can feed their babies," I said. "This is necessary for the child's survival."

The stranger stopped stroking his penis and laughed. "Com, are you spraying me again? How old are you, anyway?"

"At least fourteen years." I forgot to add the three years before we had started notching the cottonwood post in the cave.

"Yeah, I thought you were a little young for it. You've probably only drove the bone with boys."

I remained silent. I knew he was talking about the penis. I knew how the penis behaved in the middle of the night, in dreams. I knew this felt good. And I had decided that Otis had probably shared this with Malèna when they were entwined together at the end of the day and that this type of touching was what Otis meant by make love. Perhaps the stranger practiced a version of it with boys.

"You have driven it with boys, com?"

He was stroking his penis slowly.

"No."

"I can't believe it. Well, I could do you right now, if you want, so you know what it feels like. I'm getting pretty hard just talking about it."

"That's okay. I'm waiting for a wife."

"Wife!" he roared and tilted backward and slapped both thighs. His penis flopped upward. "And you don't even know how to do it with boys! Well, I myself have attained reproductive age for national service. But government sourcing sent me a bad selection. I met her at weekly meeting. She's got a tractor face and is uglier than I am. The coupling room was reserved for us. But I'll tell you, com, I'd rather drive a can of lubricant than her any day. That's why I ran away."

"What about your uncle, and a job?"

"Mixing it up and driving, com, that's what I'm after."

Gooseflesh rippled down my body. I pulled on my shorts and tied the belt tightly, setting the sheath knife to the left side. I felt as though I were outside my body, watching myself. One part of me said "run," while the other part wanted to stay on the beach and try to sort out what the stranger was talking about.

"My uncle says in the Center you can pick anyone you want and then just start doing it," he said. His arms were straight, supporting the weight of his chest. His penis had fallen to the side.

"Usually, you meet one woman who becomes your wife and then after a day's work you lie in bed together and make love," I said.

"Ha! You're spraying me again, little com! I might be from the quarry, but for sure it's not that thing you said. It's about hold on because here we go!"

The stranger lay back on the ground and rubbed his penis with both hands. At first he did this quietly, as though he were concentrating. Then, as his penis grew larger, he grunted and moaned and moved his hands faster. Suddenly, he began to groan, as though he were hurting himself. Then he was silent. He wiped his hands on his shorts and propped himself on his elbows. He smiled, showing a stupid grin. His cheeks were pink from his effort, brighter than the pustules that dotted them.

"And don't tell me you can wait for the day you do," he said.

His penis was long and limp now. Spittle was around his lips.

"I have to go," I said.

I slid my arms through the straps of my pack. I looked straight ahead and picked out a line along the shore and up to the trail that led to the footbridge.

"Where, little com?"

He stood up and licked his lips. He wasn't smiling. His thick muscles were puffed out, taut.

At first I didn't answer but started to walk up the beach. The stranger followed like a shadow.

"I have work to do," I said, not turning around. "Up the valley, the animals," I lied.

"What, with others? I thought you were alone. You better not tell them about me!"

The stranger's shrill voice drilled into the back of my head.

"What would I tell anyone about you?" I blurted over my shoulder. "That you can't even ride a bike!"

"Fucking blow-out sent me over the handlebars, com!"

I knew right away that I had made a mistake, that my mouth had opened before my brain could tell it to remain closed. I ran toward the path. The stranger followed, shouting:

"Slinging poke words at me! Stalling out, com. Backsliding. No traction. Alarm, hear me? Mixer's coming!"

He shoved me in the back, and I stumbled forward. As I recovered, he shoved me again.

"Alarm, com, hear me? You ready for it?"

I regained my balance and swung my bent legs forward as fast as I could. The stranger chased me barefoot over the footbridge, across the road, and up through the town's grid of thistle-filled streets, swearing as shards of stone and glass and bits of metal cut his feet, which slapped against the hard ground.

"Bowlegged daddy's boy. I'm gonna hammer you!"

I felt his hand close over my arm, and a sharp pain shot to my shoulder as muscle and nerve compressed against bone. I reached for my knife and drew it across his stomach, then shook off his grasp and zagged right and headed toward two demolished houses.

I sprinted into a jagged trough of debris—shattered vinyl siding, delaminated plywood, broken wallboard. Nails caught in the rubber of my sandals. Something slammed into my empty pack and sent a jolt through my spine—a piece of concrete, or a brick, maybe. Something whizzed over my head. Then I heard the stranger screaming:

"You're a reject, com! A mistake! Pliered! But some clinic bitch let you live. Next time I see you, I'll finish the operation!"

My knife seemed not to have cut him. Perhaps I'd used the dull edge of the blade. Or the stranger's skin was so thick that it wouldn't split without intense pressure.

I wove in and out and around the collapsed houses, occasionally taking advantage of stretches of clear but churned-up streets to put greater distance between us. A forested ravine led to the top of Windy Butte, and I crashed through its brush and trees, grabbing onto the fractured limbs of elms so I wouldn't slide downhill. Halfway up the butte I heard a rustling in the leaves. A grouse exploded into the air in front of me. At least it hadn't been a rattler. The sound of crashing filled my head. I slipped and fell spread out on the leafy ground of the ravine.

I listened to myself pant and didn't move until I had calmed down.

The ravine followed a corner up the butte and exited onto the prairie, on the edge of the field of wind turbines that had once powered the town. A large yellow metal bucket, rusted and with a row of big teeth, a relic of a backhoe, had been left lying tipped on its side. I crawled through a bunch of porcupine grass. There was enough space for me to sit with my legs tucked against my chest, back pressed to the cool steel, which soothed my throbbing muscles, already beginning to stiffen and ache. The wind sang across the opening of the bucket and moaned inside. The long propeller of a lone wind turbine wobbled back and forth above me. My mind was bursting, the spaces colliding one against another. There was no room for anything new.

From the yellow bucket on top of Windy Butte, I could see across the valley to Otis Butte: the band of trees spread across its flanks and up its ravines, the grassy plain extending to the horizon, and the lone trees—one of them the juniper under which Otis was buried. I focused on the one at the far left of the line and imagined Otis's spirit flowing through the sap of the branches.

As I stared at the distant tree, a new thought arose in my mind: the only way out of my fix was to kill the stranger. Until he attacked me, I had thought he would leave on his own. But crouched in the yellow bucket left behind on the prairie, I realized the real truth was that here in White Earth River he could become dependent on me to provide food and water and shelter—and perhaps conversation and sex, which if I didn't agree to would result in further assault. He had everything he needed in White Earth River. He wasn't going to leave. These were the facts.

I had never thought about killing someone. Despite Otis's stories about the murder of Sammy Goldrausch, the destruction of the town and the disappearance of its inhabitants—and the supposed roaming bands of agents ready to pick us up—we, Otis and I, had been able to avoid the murder and genocide that had swept the continent. When the machines had arrived in our town, we had hidden in the basement. Even my parents, with bellies full of *tesgüino* and venison, had probably put up more resistance than Otis had. Otis and I killed only animals for food.

Perhaps killing the stranger was a necessity, too, for my survival, though killing him wasn't the same as killing an animal. The animals of White Earth River were part of the web of life. Otis and I respected the sacrifice they made for us to live. The stranger wasn't part of this. He was a foreign species that didn't belong in the valley.

As I stared at the juniper far away on Otis Butte, I thought how Otis's life didn't offer much guidance in what to do. I remembered a story we had once read together. It was about a king who instructed his subjects to protect the kingdom from invaders and then conveniently died before any showed up. This was the portrait of Otis, a picture of unreliability.

Otis had lectured me about defending our land with my life, but he had never experienced the feelings that come with battle, how blows vibrate through the body and produce pain, how the desire to strike back makes the heart race, the body jerk, the teeth grind against each other, how words stay unformed, deep in the throat. Otis had never spoken of the urge to kill and how quickly it can take over. He knew nothing about plotting murder.

I decided that my knife had cut the stranger because I remembered feeling tissue give way when I sliced his stomach. Perhaps he would lose enough blood to become weakened, perhaps enough to die, before I had to finish him.

I knew that I couldn't fight him face to face for more than a minute. He was too strong, even in a weakened state. I remembered the tightness that came from walking long distances and squatting all day in the garden—always in the tendon above the heel. If I could sever this cord, the stranger would hobble on one leg for a moment before falling to the ground in pain, at which point I could stab him or club him to death as I did deer.

"You have to get close to kill it," I remembered Otis saying before I clubbed my first deer. I would have only one chance to cripple the stranger. I would need to sharpen the machete, first with the file, then with the whetstone. I would crouch low and attack as a mountain lion did.

This plan made my mouth parched. I needed something to satisfy my thirst until it could be quenched by action. Embedded in a tuft of grass, I found a rock left behind by the glacier. With a bent, rusty bolt from a fallen wind turbine, I chipped off a flake and placed it on my tongue. I curled up inside the yellow metal bucket and slept fitfully, sucking on the piece of granite until daylight arrived and warmed my stiff body.

The machete was meant for hacking down plants, although occasionally I used its blunt spine on small animals and once on a doe. After testing the honed blade, I slipped my hand through the leather strap and gripped the wooden handle. The soreness in my arm and back reminded me to act with speed, to swing the tool as though I were clearing the field of dried cornstalks. Although I could have eaten and drunk, I didn't. An empty stomach would keep me light for a quick strike.

The doors to the boathouse were open, and I advanced in a crouched position, low with feet apart for stability and my right arm raised for a sharp downward swing. As my eyes adjusted to the dim light, I smelled the stench of vomit. On the floor lay the stranger, wearing a life preserver. Two more were draped over his legs. His body twitched. The critical tendon in his leg wasn't exposed. I took a step forward.

"I'm sick, com," the stranger said.

If I had had a club, I perhaps could have smashed his skull, a blunt injury that is almost bloodless. But I couldn't tolerate seeing the gash and blood that the machete would inflict. The thought of splitting open his forehead made me sweat, and combined with the sour air from the stranger's vomit, I retched and spit bile on the floor. The stranger didn't seem to hear me or see the machete, quivering in the air over him, and I lowered it.

The one aspect of killing that I never adjusted to was determining the number of blows necessary to kill an animal and then waiting for it to die. I was thankful for not having to figure this out for the stranger and said the prayer that Otis offered up whenever we trapped or killed an animal. "We accept this and offer thanks in return." The stranger would soon die; between his sickness and the knife wound, I doubted whether he'd last more than a couple of days.

"I hate them, com, the heaves. They open up that cut you gave me. The first time I fought them and passed out. When I came to, I sat up and spewed all over myself. I have the shits, too. I've been doing it over the edge of the dock. Sorry."

I recalled Otis's speeches about germs and how we owed our health to lack of contact with other humans. Now that I was no longer at risk of the stranger's physical threat, I faced the disease and contamination he could pass on. Even if I killed him, his germs would still be left behind.

"I'm so weak. My coms in the quarry said that if I ran away, I'd die. Runaways never return."

If I did nothing, once the stranger died I'd need to burn down the boathouse to rid our land of his body and germs. But if I could take him away now, sail him down the lake, and leave him on a shore to die, I wouldn't have to worry about that task.

"They don't even find the bodies. They send agents out looking for runaways, but they never bring any back. You think they just kill them when they find them, leave them dead and alone? Shit, I'm always around people, working. Do you know what it's like to be alone?"

"You need a clinic," I said to him.

"They'd probably arrest me. I used my hammer. My father was drunk. It made a bad sound."

"We'll have to sail to the Center."

"Can't you just give me a shot or a pill?"

"In the Center there's a clinic. They'll give you something. And contact your uncle, too."

"He won't be happy about that."

"He'll be able to help you."

"He's not going to be happy."

"I'll get the canoe ready."

"Don't be gone long, com. Five minutes, promise?"

"Okay, five minutes."

The stranger closed his eyes. Five minutes, I thought. What was that? Four more than the "just a minute" that Otis used to say when I asked for something?

Otis had told me that the Center was east, a fast train ride in days when the spur line from White Earth River connected to the main east–west train line, but whether it was possible to sail to the Center I didn't know. It didn't matter. We weren't going there, only to a distant shore, a resting place, I'd tell the stranger. I'd make him a cup of nightshade. For his stomach, I'd tell him. After he fell asleep, I'd paddle away.

I gathered only a few things: a bladder of well water, the tin cup, the rest of the sunflower seeds, a stalk of broccoli, some leaves of kale, and the nightshade, its roots, stem, and leaves wrapped in a piece of plastic tarp so no part of the plant touched my skin.

As I walked back to the boathouse from the garden, I began to worry about whether the stranger might regain strength and try to attack me or run away. I had the machete and the canoe paddle. But I wanted some cord to bind his wrists, or maybe his feet, if I needed to.

The yellow rope was in a tangle where I had left it, more faded than when I had used it to haul Otis to his grave. I coiled the cord and slung it over my shoulder and turned to go, but the branches of the juniper caught my eye. From the way they stirred, whipping back and forth, I knew that Otis's spirit was angry, but what could it tell me that would be of any use?

"I might be the last one here, but I'm the first to do this," I said to the tree.

The branches of the juniper didn't move. Otis couldn't argue with that. He was hiding in the tree, entwined with Malèna. I brushed my hair from my face and gathered it behind my head. "I'm taking your ribbon, too. You don't need it anymore." For strength, I thought. But when I searched the low branches for the ribbon, I couldn't find it. Nor was it lying in the grass. He has it, I thought. He'd found Malèna and she'd braided his hair and tied it with the red ribbon. Or maybe the overhand knot with which I had attached it to the branch had come undone, and the wind had blown the ribbon away.

His shirt had bloodstains on it from where his wound had leaked, and putting on the life jacket made him wince. His face was white, even the pustules and welts from the goose, as though blood had ceased to circulate to his head. He shivered as he walked down the boat ramp. Stomach cramps caused him to double over and drop to his knees and gag.

"It hurts when I puke," he said, looking up at me. "You shouldn't have cut me. I didn't deserve that."

He sat back on his heels and spit and wiped his mouth with the back of his hand.

Of course you deserved it, I wanted to say but instead said, "Drink some water. It'll help pass the germs." Then I poured a trickle from the rubber bladder into his mouth to let him know that I wasn't afraid of him, that I'd cut him again if I had to.

He shook his head at the red canoe, which the current had pushed parallel to the dock, and staggered as he lifted a leg to step into the bow, sitting on the bottom, not the seat. A gloss of sweat coated his forehead, and he hugged his legs to his chest as he rocked to and fro trying to calm himself. The canoe sent ripples out across the shallow water.

I hauled the rigging from the boathouse and arranged our packs forward of the stern seat. With one end of the yellow rope, I lashed them to the mast thwart; the other end I saved to restrain the stranger, if needed.

I had never paddled, much less sailed, a loaded canoe. As we drifted in the current, I saw that it was sitting low in the water. Here, upriver from the bay and lake, shrubs and trees protected us from strong breezes, but out on open water I knew the wind would kick up. I might have to fight to make headway. Gusts would be stronger later in the afternoon, too.

I looked at the sky. The upper layers were streaked with clouds. They could go either way: build up and lower to the ground or dissipate. A hint of sun would have reassured me that the day would end with a red sunset and not a storm. Warmer air, too, would have taken the bite out of the breeze. But neither was present that morning.

I kneeled on a life preserver and leaned into the paddling, pleased at the distance I generated with each stroke, which I ended in a satisfying J-shape to keep us heading in a straight line. The geese nesting on the peninsula were quiet as we passed. Perhaps they understood my risk. I didn't talk to the stranger, who sat facing forward, his arms locked around his legs, his head down until he needed to see the horizon to prevent himself from vomiting.

Where the river entered the bay, I beached the canoe and walked through the silt and up a grassy terrace for a better view. The stranger stayed in the canoe and threw up over the side. The wind flattened the surface of the water and stirred ripples into patches of chop. I dug a handful of sunflower seeds from my pocket and chewed them into a mush, not bothering to spit out the pulverized shells.

"Might be a little rough," I said and pushed the canoe into the bay, tipping it as I stepped inside. The motion set the stranger off balance and made him call out and shift his weight to compensate. There, I thought, he's scared.

"It'd be better if we were walking," he said.

"This is the fastest way."

The wind created pressure on the sail, and I could feel the stress through the rudder and the mainsheet line, which dug into my hand as we tacked across the bay. Under the low clouds the water was black, appearing deeper, more difficult to read, than it was on a sunny day. Spray broke over the bow and hit the stranger's face, which made him twitch and risk letting go of the gunwales to wipe his eyes. Coming about, the canoe almost stalled. As chop hit the hull and wind thrashed the sail, I saw that I would have to bring greater momentum in to change directions.

I ran out the last tack across the bay and sailed into the open waters of Lake Sakakawea. Wind buffeted the canoe. We rode up and down swells. Gusts slapped small, sharp waves over the gunwales and forced me to spill wind from the sail. The shock of the water soaking his lap made the stranger gasp and rise up. I shouted for him to sit down. There was too much to pay attention to, the force of the wind, the size and timing of the swells, the balance of the canoe. Rather than coming about and zigzagging down lake, I held the tack and headed toward a point of land in the shadow of a huge cement bridge abutment from which terns and gulls scouted the lake.

I passed close to shore but didn't stop. The stranger, no longer capable of suppressing a spasm, vomited into the lake.

"It's those waves. If it were calm, I'd be fine," he said, turning and looking under the sail to make eye contact with me.

"No, it's the germs," I said, not looking at him but straight ahead at the swells.

"It's the waves. If we were walking, I'd be okay."

"River water, you never know what's in it."

I hoped that reminding the stranger of his illness and the roughness of the water would keep his stomach upset. It would take too much time to go ashore and boil the nightshade or convince him that the raw leaves would cure his ills. Anyway, the bridge spanned the lake, which would make it easy for him to find his way among the deserted farm roads or the unused train line back to White Earth River. I didn't want to leave him yet, either, in these sailing conditions; in the rough water I felt safer with him in the canoe, if his only value was ballast against the waves.

The sail slackened as the canoe nosed into the leeward shadow of the bridge. The lake narrowed. Broad plateaus extended to the north and south, and their bluffs absorbed the wind, causing it to blow unevenly through this cut in the earth. I dropped the sail and let us drift. My hand had become numb from the wrap of the mainsheet line around my palm; my arm, stiff from serving as a rigid extension of the tiller. I dug sunflower seeds from my pocket and chewed them into a mash. The rigging squeaked. The canoe turned sideways, then around. I massaged the circulation back into my hand.

"We almost to the Center?" the stranger asked.

He leaned forward. I thought he would vomit again, but he seemed to be looking down into the water.

"You see a fish?" I asked.

"A big shape passed."

"A pike, a paddlefish, maybe."

"It was dark. Like a shadow."

It was too overcast for shadows, but I didn't correct the stranger.

"We have just a little farther to go," I said and took up the paddle.

"Maybe they can help you find your father. At the clinic."

"They might arrest me."

"Maybe because you're helping me they won't. We can stay with my uncle. He won't be happy about it, but he'll come around. What'd your father do?"

"You mean work?"

"Yeah."

"I'm not sure. I was a baby when he disappeared."

"Well, he had to have done something."

Otis had never said what my parents did before coming to White Earth River. I couldn't imagine them living in the Center, but the stranger's suggestion made me consider this.

The slow rhythm of dipping the paddle blade into the water and pulling was a relief after the tension and speed of being blown over the water. I could've paddled for the rest of the afternoon. We passed finger-shaped coves pointing deep inland. Could I have abandoned the stranger in one of these? We had come far enough that it would be unlikely for him to be able to find his way back to White Earth River. But I didn't like the thought of being enclosed, trapped in a narrow channel, and sitting out the afternoon with the stranger until the nightshade put him to sleep. I wanted to arrive on a wide beach at the end of the day, make a fire, boil some tea, and then slip away and drift until daylight.

When the lake widened again, it seemed as though we had entered an ocean, although from Otis's geography lessons I knew that this wasn't possible. Still, I dipped my hand in the cool water and licked my fingers to make sure the water wasn't salty.

Waves seemed to grow out of the lake, rise up into little hills, and then spill forth their white foam. The waves never flattened or disappeared but continued to reappear, again and again, in the same place. In the distance were short, gray bluffs, perhaps the end of the lake. Surely I could reach them by dusk.

I fought the plastic tiller to steer the canoe in quartering movements into the waves and spilled wind from the sail to control our speed. The sudden ascent up the slope of a wave followed by dropping down into the trough scared me, and I ordered the stranger to turn face down and to push against the front thwart to stabilize the canoe. He cried out as he threw himself toward the bow when we crashed over a swell. The wound in his stomach had opened up again.

The gusts bent the carbon fiber mast and snapped the boom up and down against its line. The monotony of steering, cresting through the white foam, and aligning the craft to take on the next wave began to tire and dull me. I shuffled my weight more slowly from side to side and leaned over the gunwale recklessly as I tried to balance the boat. We seemed to be suspended in the lake, unmoving, despite the bluffs on the horizon appearing to become larger and closer.

As we entered the middle of this endless sea, the tiller bent at its attachment point with the rudder. The tiller wasn't designed to sail in high wind. It was intended for a morning of fun on flat water on a calm day. As the tiller bent and then snapped, I lost the ability to steer and couldn't prevent the canoe from turning downwind. I felt myself giving up, surrendering to the forces of the lake. I was exhausted. What more could I do than let out the main sheet and hope we could survive the run toward whichever shore the wind chose for us?

I felt a rush of cool water sweep over my back and fill the canoe. The stranger jerked and cried out when the cold water hit him. I gripped the broken tiller and let go of the main sheet. The stranger caught the boom as it whipped past him. "Don't!" I shouted too late. The wind caught the sail, the canoe drifted broadside, and a swell, like a gentle hand coming from below, rolled us silently into the lake. The mast fell like a leafless sapling, and the surface of the lake absorbed the sail without a sound.

At first we didn't speak. I treaded water beside the canoe, bobbing up and down with the swells, letting cool water wash over my face and into my parched mouth. The flapping sail was finally quiet, which calmed me. It wasn't so bad, being in the water. At least the battle with the wind was over.

The stranger was in a blue life vest zipped to the chin yet he thrashed and gasped at the shock of being dumped into the lake. I grabbed a paddle floating nearby and wedged it under the yellow rope, which still secured our packs to the thwarts. The water bladder had come loose and floated on the surface like a dead fish. I tucked that under a strand of the yellow rope as well.

I remembered the words of the "Safe Boating" booklet: "When in trouble, stay with your craft until help arrives." "Stay with the boat," I shouted to the stranger but not the rest, because I knew that no one was going to save us, that we had to rescue ourselves. The stranger continued to thrash but didn't move any closer to the boat. I clutched the gunwale of the half-submerged canoe and kicked my feet to tread water.

"You're wearing yourself out. Get to the boat," I shouted.

"I can't swim."

"Paddle with your hands toward the boat. Like this."

I demonstrated the stroke.

"I'm sinking."

"Don't struggle. Let the life vest keep you up. Paddle toward me with your hands."

"It's pulling me down, com. The vest. It's heavy."

The stranger beat his arms through the water, but his body didn't rise up. A swell washed over his head. He spit out water and coughed.

"Take it off! Now!" I screamed over the wind.

The stranger held his breath and unzipped the vest, dipping below the surface as he struggled to pull his arms free. He rose, flailing against the surface of the water and coughing. The life vest drifted downward like a giant blue fish diving for prey. A moment later it was gone. The vest seemed to have been filled with lead sinkers; perhaps it was too old to work.

"Paddle back to me. Use your hands. Now!" I shouted.

"I can't." His voice was weak.

"Yes, you can. Watch me."

I let go of the canoe to show him, but a swell lifted me up and I grabbed onto the canoe again. The stranger floated down the slope of the wave as he worked his arms in circles, propelling himself upward but not toward the canoe.

"Wait! I'll throw you a line."

I untangled the loose ends of the yellow rope from the thwart and tossed it to the stranger. It fell short.

"Damn! I'll push the canoe toward you!"

I pulled myself hand-over-hand along the gunwale until I was at the stern. I tried to frog kick the boat forward, but the drag of the sail acted as an anchor. I waited for a swell, to time my kicks with the push of the wave, but the froth washed over me and the canoe didn't move any closer to the stranger.

A swell now separated us, and I could see the stranger only when the peak of a wave raised him up.

"Com! Com!" I shouted the only name I knew for the stranger. "I'm swimming to you."

Energy surged through my body, and I plowed through a trough and up the slope of a swell and down its backside to within a couple arms' lengths of the stranger. His head dipped below the surface and then bobbed up again as he worked his arms.

"I'm sinking, com."

"No, take my hand!"

I extended one hand and treaded water with the other. The stranger grabbed onto my forearm with both hands and dragged me toward him, pulling me under the water. I shook loose from his grasp and kicked him away. He floated up as a wave rushed over him.

"Don't fight! Let me tow you!"

The stranger dropped below the surface and rose coughing before he slipped down again. I grabbed his right hand. He was heavy but didn't struggle. I waited for a whitecap to pass and then started to swim toward the canoe. When I reached the mast, I stopped and crimped his hand around the pole. He let out a weak cough and drifted below the surface. A swell passed over him, and his hand slipped into the water.

"Hold on!"

I squeezed his hand around the mast again and treaded water behind him. I forced his other hand to the mast and covered both of his hands with mine. Pressed tight against the stranger's back, I couldn't tread water. I tried to maneuver my body so I could, but in every position my legs became entangled with the stranger's legs. If I hung there, behind him, my hands pressing down on his, I would start to sink, too. I couldn't keep holding my breath. If I could loop the yellow rope around him . . .

"Keep holding on. I'm right beside you," I said.

I let go of the stranger's hands. A swell raised us up, and his hands slipped from the mast. He seemed to drop down a hole. His fingers, still bent in an open clasp, were the last to disappear. I probed the cool water with my feet, reached down and searched for him with my hands, and then I dove. One stroke, two strokes—all around the water was cold. I opened my eyes but saw nothing, only darkness. I resurfaced, gasping for air, and then dove again. And then again. And then once more. Then I gave up. The stranger was gone.

I had tried to save him. The currents of the Missouri flowing through the lake had taken him. But they didn't take me. Something had protected me. This is why I lived and the stranger died.

My knife hadn't slid out of its sheath when we capsized, and I hacked at the rigging and pulled the mast and boom free. The canoe righted itself. I watched the mast and its triangle of white cloth drift over a swell and float out of sight. I tried using the inner tube to bail out the canoe, but for every bladder of water I emptied, another wave deposited twice as much. I tried to swim the swamped canoe up waves and down into troughs, frog kicking, arms stretched out from the stern. The prow acted as a small sail and helped me along. Cold crept into my body. My muscles cramped. I rested, a hand hanging on to each gunwale, and floated.

A dark cloud hung below layers of gray. I hoped I would drift to shore before the sky let loose with lightning and rain. I tightened my grip on the canoe and let the cool water of Lake Sakakawea wash over me. My body rose and fell with the swells; my chest bumped against the useless rudder. I began to kick again when the drizzle started.

PART IV: PARSHALL BAY (ALONE)

The wind pushed the canoe toward a spit of sand. When my feet touched the silty bottom, a wave of silent relief flowed through my body. What a surprise, what a gift. At first I couldn't believe it. I waded to shore, and a swell nudged the water-filled canoe forward. It was too heavy, filled with water, to tow above the high-water line, but I feared that left alone, it would drift away.

I had survived, that's all that mattered. Even though I didn't know where I was or how I'd get home—or even to mainland—the little island was a better place than where I had been. I said a prayer of thanks. Surely Otis had been watching me and urging the spirit world to protect me.

I rocked the canoe back and forth to dump its watery contents back into the lake and then hauled it up the shore. The stranger's pack was still tied to a thwart next to mine. He hadn't had many belongings: the two mason's hammers, a T-shirt, a pair of shorts, and a plastic water bottle. I didn't want to be reminded of him and so slung the pack into the lake. The weight of his mason's hammers sunk it.

I walked to the top of the spit. The distance to the mainland wasn't far. In fair weather it would have been an easy sail or a long paddle. Although I didn't look forward to setting out again, the thought that I could make it to shore gave me hope and let me ignore my exhaustion.

The wind caught the bow, now no longer weighted down by the stranger, and pushed the canoe off course. I tried to fight this, but my enthusiasm and energy drained away to weariness. My strokes became sloppy. The paddle knocked against the hull, and my knuckles banged on the gunwale. I let the slope of one swell push me part of the way up the next before I tried to paddle over the top.

I was confined once again to a world of swells, with little sense of escaping them. It was a mistake not to have spent the night on the spit, what now seemed to have been my last chance for land, although a small bit of it. Then, in the next moment, as though a sheet had parted, an inlet appeared. The shore was not far. I was delivered. My spirits lightened. I paddled harder.

Within the protection of the bay, the wind died down and the swells flattened. The sound of my paddle dipping into the water and hitting the hull filled the air. Grasslands stretched to the north and forests and fields spread to the south. I had returned to a seemingly familiar world.

I paddled toward what looked like a cluster of bare white tree trunks, half-fallen and leaning into the water, as though the roots had become waterlogged and caused them to topple over and die. As I came closer, though, I saw that these weren't trees but the masts of sailboats tilting skyward. The boats had been left behind and settled into the silty bottom of the lake as the water level had fallen. Tethers of rotting rope connected the boats to a beached dock. A long wooden walkway snaked through grass and cottonwood saplings to a cement boat ramp and landing and, farther up the shore, to a low cement block building. When the canoe scraped against bottom, I stepped into the cool shallows and towed the boat up onto the shore.

I was sure no one lived here. The brightwork on the sailboats had corroded. Sun had beat down on the hulls and decks and dulled the white plastic. The trim had weathered, too, its varnish having peeled years ago, leaving the wood gray and cracked. Only the halyard cables, vibrating against the aluminum masts in a type of song, suggested life.

I didn't want to stay on the beach in the cool rain. It was almost dark. I needed shelter, a place where I could make a fire and dry out. The windowless cement block building turned out to be a boathouse, but at that point I had had my fill of boathouses and would have rather slept outside in the rain than in this dark, cold building.

I followed a path through a grove of tall, evenly spaced cottonwoods whose canopy shaded out any trace of an understory. As I walked over the damp soil, the leaves overhead trembled. The sound, rather than comforting me as it usually did, seemed to warn me to rush through these woods as quickly as possible. I crossed an asphalt road and headed up a street lined with pines and elms, trees that I had never seen growing together. Midway up the hill on my right, a crushed stone path disappeared between two rows of tightly spaced junipers. This seemed to be a secret passageway of sorts, perhaps one that led to a safe place.

The path ended in a clearing before an abandoned single-story house. Vegetation had taken over the house. A mat of dark-green leaves with yellow borders had crawled up the walls and onto the flat roof of the house. A row of shrubs with small, shiny green leaves and orange berries blocked the high, wide windows just below the roof. On each side of the door were short trees with crooked trunks and branches that had grown into each other. Dried pink flowers lingered on the tips of their stems. The roots of a large tree, with bark in strips, had caused the flat stone entrance path to heave and break apart. I couldn't identify any of this vegetation, and its disorder troubled me.

Above the door handle was a square metal lever. I pressed this, and, with a slight push, the door opened. Cool damp air and the musty odor of mold filled my nose. A window almost as tall as the ceiling lined the far side of the room and provided the only light to navigate through the brown-and-green-streaked walls of the short entry corridor.

The floor was stone, and a carpet of muted roses, their blossoms full with red, orange, and yellow petals, covered much of it. A metal-framed bench with brown cushions lined one edge of the rug, which squished as I stepped on a corner. Above, on the ceiling, a brown stain showed where the roof had leaked—like in the back of the cave where water seeped through soil and rock, darkening the cottonwood timbers. At one end of the room was the kitchen. A vine-covered window above the sink barely admitted light. On the other end of the room was a wall of bookshelves with a desk and monitor built into them.

Behind the house was an expanse of sand, dotted with neat piles of rocks and the blackened remains of burned trees. Over this landscape arched a lattice structure as tall as the house and constructed of six-sided interlocking windows. A patch of green, moss or grass—I couldn't tell—grew in the shade of an elm tree that had fallen and punched a hole through the structure. Something had happened here, a fire, it looked like.

I raised a latch on the tall, wide window and slid it open. It was a door, after all. The decayed wooden planking of the deck squeaked under my weight. The emptiness reminded me of my town. The warm, moldy air under the false sky of the lattice of windows made me cough, and I went back into the house.

As my eyes adjusted to the dimness of the room, I noticed four wooden masks in a row on a wall. They seemed to meet my stare and scowl. They had been carved with a knife, with most of the cuts in the wood not having been smoothed but left irregular and jagged. The open mouths were decorated with shells and feathers and pieces of metal and leather. White had been painted around the eyes. Only the cheeks and brows had been polished, and these caught the faint light coming through the door. I looked out again at the barren land, trying to see it as these wooden faces might. They seemed to be angry about what had happened.

I decided not to sleep in the house for fear of disturbing the masks. Instead, under the lattice of windows next to a charred stump, I made a fire with the rotting deck planks. Smoke settled around me, and the smell of it and the burning wood reminded me of the cave. I collected water to boil—I had no tea to add to it—from a down-spout and chewed the remainder of my sunflower seeds into a warm mash. I wanted to lie down, get out of my wet clothes, and sleep. In the house I found two blankets, a thin one, which I slept on, and a feather-filled one, which I covered myself with.

I lay beside the dying fire and listened to the rain hitting the windows above me. The sound reminded me of rain falling on the tin roof of the monorail platform. In the darkness rounds of thunder passed over the prairie, and I waited for jags of lightning to brighten the sky. Although I was lying on my back, resting, my body seemed to be in the lake, floating in the water. The sensation of rising up and down with the swells filled me. The clammy blanket on my chest re-minded me of pressing against the taut muscles of the stranger's back, feeling his body's warmth through his wet T-shirt while I clasped his cold, water-softened hands over the mast. When I rolled to my side to free myself of this feeling, I felt the stranger slipping away, bumping once against my chest before vanishing into the lake's depth. Not even my legs, vigorously treading water, felt him pass. I shuddered and curled into a ball, with my back to the masks.

I woke in the morning haunted by a dream: Animals with four legs, long bushy tails, and gray-black matted hair were prowling the prairie. They might have been dogs or coyotes but seemed to resemble most the wolves I had read about in stories. Their heads were raised in the air as though they were howling, but instead of a howl, a mournful song, sadder than any Otis had ever sung, came out of their mouths. Their sides were shredded and ratty looking, their coats scarred with oozing wounds, as though another animal had attacked and bit them—pulled off fur and tissue to eat strips of flesh. Some of them had ribs exposed. Despite all this, though, they had kept singing.

I didn't know what to make of the dream, but it began to inhabit me and fill the space in my mind that the stranger had previously occupied.

A humid, cool cloud seemed to engulf the lattice and make the sky thick and gray, low enough to touch, if the plastic windows hadn't been there. Rain fell through the hole in the roof, and a wet breeze stirred the air. My whole body was sore, as if the wooden faces had slunk down off the wall during the night and bitten me all over with their angry mouths.

Despite living in moisture and wetness, I was thirsty. There were cooking pots in the kitchen of the abandoned house. A small one I used to collect water from the downspout. On the desk in the bookshelves was a notebook, with pages filled with drawings and lines of formulae that I didn't understand but used to start the damp kindling for a fire. While I waited for water to boil, I searched my pockets for sunflower seeds. Only two remained in a deep corner of a front pocket. I would need more than that to get home, especially if I were stranded at this house until the weather cleared. And without a sail, just how long would it take to paddle back to White Earth River?

In the bottom of my pack I found the broccoli, which I tossed into the pot, along with wilted kale, which had already lost most of its flavor. I was careful not to unwrap the nightshade. Dampness had softened and opened my blisters. I might poison myself if I touched the herb.

I sat close to the fire and smelled the sharp aroma of the broccoli as its steam rose in the close air. I could walk home, perhaps finding the monorail line to our town, but leaving the canoe behind seemed to be unwise—the windy passage up the lake was the only route home that I was sure of. Although the swells and the cold currents had terrified me, I knew I could trace the current, pulsing beneath me, back to White Earth River. Once the rain ceased, the swells would flatten out. If I got as far as the bridge, I could rest. Cross the lake there and then follow the shoreline until I entered White Earth Bay. If paddling wore me out, I could cross the bridge on foot. Perhaps a road would lead to White Earth River. Perhaps walking would allow me to search inland for my parents—I hadn't seen any towns on the lake's shore. Perhaps they had escaped to another river valley. But were my parents farmers? Hadn't they lived in Bismarck before White Earth River? Maybe agents had realized they were best suited to city life and relocated them to the Center. Perhaps the stranger was right: I might find them there. Maybe the risk of being arrested was the cost of finding them.

I began searching the cabinets for left-behind food and water jugs. Whichever route I took, to the Center or White Earth River, I'd need to carry water and food. A drawer was filled with silver packets with the letters MRG across the front in black, with an illustration of an arm, flexed to show bulging muscles. The stranger had spoken of MRGs, so I assumed this was the type of food he ate. The first packet I picked up had the word PROTEIN written under the arm. That's what I needed to paddle to the Center, muscles like the ones in the picture.

The hard bar of protein was sweet but difficult to chew and salty, which made me thirstier. In a cabinet near the floor I was lucky to find several clear glass bottles filled with what I first thought was an emergency supply of water.

The labels on the bottles contained a drawing of a large, bright green plant with pointed leaves, with a yellow sun overhead in a blue sky. In black cursive were the words: "In praise of Agave, Tequila, spirit of the Ancients." I didn't know that tequila contained alcohol, like the *tesgüino* my father used to drink. When I unscrewed the cap and inhaled the liquid's musky aroma, I wondered if it might be poisonous, although who would pour poison into such beautiful bottles and keep a cabinet full of them in his kitchen, I asked myself.

I sipped the tequila. It was smooth and thick in my mouth. I swallowed and felt my throat and then my stomach burn. I thought I had made a fatal mistake, but soon pleasing warmth spread through my body. I took a longer drink and waited for another shot of heat. I tried to swallow a mouthful but choked and blew a mist of liquid out my nose.

"Whoa!" I said, and then began coughing. I sat down on the bench facing the bookshelves and rubbed my nose until the fire in my nostrils subsided.

Despite my damp clothes, for the first time in two days I felt warm. I sipped more tequila and stared at the masks on the wall. I began to feel loose and happy. Time slowed down. I settled into the brown leather cushions on the bench.

I alternated between looking at the masks and looking at the burnt landscape out the back door. There had to be a connection. The masks had to know something about what had happened. Every time I returned my focus to the masks, it seemed that their expression had changed. I began to feel that they were watching me, that they had decided I was the one who had burned down the trees.

"I didn't do that," I said to the masks and nodded toward the backyard, "so don't frown at me. And I didn't kill the stranger, so you can't blame me for that, either."

Their expressions softened, as though they were saying, "Oh, no, we didn't think that, we were just wondering why you were here."

"Just gathering provisions before I leave," I said to them.

"No rush," their expressions seemed to say. "We're happy to have a visitor. Stay as long as you like."

I raised my glass to them in thanks. I liked the taste of the tequila, the woody smell, and the sense of wholeness that it gave me. I drank more.

"Hey, let me sing you something," I said to the masks, beginning the song that the wolves had sung: "Hi-ne-a, hi-ne-a, hi-ne-a. . . ."

I wanted Otis's spirit to hear me. I wanted to tell him about my dream. But the faces were right there, looking at me and asking, "Yes?"

"The wolves . . . they were behind the house last night. Did you hear them? Right next to me. Singing in my ear. Hi-ne-a, hi-ne-a, hi-ne-a. . . . And you," I pointed the glass at them, "I felt you, biting me in the ass!" I laughed, and the masks laughed along with me.

"My grandfather. My grandfather, he knew about the currents. That's why he took quick baths and never learned to swim and didn't wade out into the river. He knew what they were up to even though he tried to hide from them. The basement . . . Ha! The Missouri River. It's still down there even though you can't see it! I felt it the first time I sailed into the lake!"

I took another swallow. I began to suspect that a connection existed between the masks and the currents of the Missouri, and that they, the masks, knew what had happened on the lake and that the currents had somehow signaled to the masks that they would push me toward the house where the masks lived.

"Hey, tell us a story!" I screamed at the shelves of books.

I set the bottle on the floor and staggered to the bookshelf and opened a thick book. It contained page after page of diagrams—jumbles of lines, rows of numbers, funny symbols, and an occasional arrow. "E-lec-trical En-gin-eer-ing," I sounded out the title. I dropped it onto the floor and giggled at the thump it made.

"Did you hear that?" I asked the masks. "Like pounding corn! You know about pounding corn?"

I liked the sound of books slapping against the stone tiles, and the floor quickly became littered with dense, unreadable texts, some with broken spines and others with covers attached by only a few threads.

"Useless books!"

I laughed and continued yanking volume after volume from the shelves and watched as they spilled onto the wet rug. The heavier books I raised over my head and threw them onto the stone floor to see how loud of a sound I could make. The masks didn't seem to like what I was doing with the books. They began to scowl.

"What? You don't think this is funny?" I asked them.

Their lack of a response told me that, no, they didn't think it was funny. This made me sad, and I looked down at the mess I had created. A book with a photograph of a desert landscape on its cover caught my eye. A type of butte, not unlike the buttes above White Earth River, was in the background. Holding this volume open, I stumbled back and forth, circling around as I tried to sit down, and fell backwards and landed with a wet squish on one of the rug's damp rose petals.

"Whoa! You gotta see this!" I shouted to the masks and held up the book. It contained photos of deserts, all taken in the late afternoon sun, when the earth was in position so the sun could rake across the land.

"Hey, where's the sun now?" I asked the masks. "Maybe you can call it out!"

I looked at the cool light draining through the glass door. I propped the book open against a metal leg of the bench, so a warm, sunny landscape rose up from the floor.

There had to be other picture books on the shelves. I'd decorate the room with them!

But the next one I pulled from the shelf was only a gardening manual, not unlike the two we had in the cave that Otis had made me read, often several times, as we tried to figure out how to prevent pests from devouring our crops.

Slips of paper left between the pages of this one guided me through chapters on greenhouse construction, desert gardens, and drainage. Some of the text was underlined, and on various pages someone had written notes: "Who cares about melting ice caps, rising sea levels, tropical storms, failing dams, floods? Those climate change jerks got it all wrong. We're gonna fry! Forest fires, scorched earth, drought, dust bowls. The desert will do us in!"

On the bottom of one page was scrawled: "Torch the forest, crank up the heat, blow it all around, do the calculations, become vindicated!"

I read the notes several times and then shouted in a gruff voice, the way I imagined the person who had written these words, a man, of course, would speak: "Torch the forest, crank up the heat, blow it all around!"

The sound of my voice made me laugh, and I recited this line a number of times to the masks, as though I were delivering it to a chunky-mouthed audience, who, in return, were laughing, "Haw, haw, haw," their big loose teeth rattling against each other. But then, the laughter stopped and a chant began, a guttural word that sounded like "Guilty!"

"I told you I didn't do it!" I shouted at them. "I'm a gardener! I don't burn down forests!"

The man had burned up the trees, I screamed. And perhaps had died in the fire in the backyard. Or maybe the masks banished him, forced him to sail off into Lake Sakakawea and then capsized him, so the currents could punish him, as they had perhaps punished the stranger for killing his father.

"Make sure no one else gets his hands on this one!" I shook the book at the masks and then put it back on the shelf.

A thin, flimsy booklet lay open on the floor. A grainy black-and-white photo showed a man walking barefoot along a mountain trail and leading a mule with bulging sacks lashed across its back. I picked up the booklet. "Farmers of the Sierra Madre Occidental" was printed in black across a soft blue cover. Two bands of wire held together what was little more than a handful of paper folded in half.

The masks had seemed to shut up, knowing that they couldn't get rid of me the way they had the man who burnt down the trees in the backyard. The room became quiet, and I settled onto the dark leather cushions, which gave a moist sigh as I collapsed into them.

The farmer in the photograph had a tanned face similar to mine, although his was lined with wrinkles. His hair was black, like mine, and his pants and shirt were baggy and dirty, like my clothes. He was not smiling but looked fearful. Underneath the photograph was written: "Bringing corn to Ojachichi, Chihuahua state, Mexico."

I began reading the booklet, a doctor's account of the year he had spent in a remote Tarahumara village in the Sierra Madre Occidental while he set up a rural clinic. Although most of the story concerned the difficulties of living in primitive conditions, there were also long passages about the friends he had made, the people standing beside their houses, fields, and animals in the photographs. A map of the area contained the same names as the ones I found in the text and captions. I sounded out these words in slurred speech, not knowing how to pronounce the words correctly.

"They're not going to make it," Otis had always said whenever I had asked about people living in other countries. "They can't grow enough food. Surpluses on the open market vanished before we starting building the Center. No fuel for transport. Starvation, disease, bad weather, drought, and war will finish everyone off." But Mexico was different. Like Canada, it was part of the North American continental government. Though its population had been culled, the doctor's study proved that these farmers of the Sierra Madre Occidental had survived and escaped relocation.

In the last years of his life, Otis had tried to reconstruct the story of his father's ancestors but had stumbled when I had asked where his father's family originated, abruptly ending his tale by saying, "Our people have always been here," meaning along the Missouri

117

River, "since the beginning of time," his voice rising to an angry silence, as though he were mad at himself for not being able to figure out the history of his supposed Hidatsa roots.

But that was Otis's story, not mine. I wasn't Hidatsa. My father *had* to come from what used to be Mexico. My resemblance to the farmers was no coincidence. And that day, drunk in the house of the masks and surrounded by the slick pages of textbooks in the damp, cool room, I could see what must have happened: my family originated in a high desert plain in Mexico where the days were warm; one of the members, a man, delivered a load of corn to a distant market and stayed there; years later his son took a sack of corn to another market farther away still; another son, many generations after that, arrived, perhaps with a wife and children, in Bismarck; and eventually another son, my father, Javier, met my mother, Maria, and they married. To find my ancestors wasn't a matter of reciting a fake family history but of simply walking in the right direction, south, until I came to the landscape that resembled the one in this photograph. My family hadn't died of hunger. The government hadn't relocated or eradicated them. They lived safely in the mountains. They had their own clinic and knew how to grow crops in a way that perhaps everyone else had forgotten. They didn't use bicycles or canoes. They walked the land. I was the last of these people, not of Otis's people.

A space opened in my mind. I tucked the blue booklet in the waistband of my shorts and struggled to my feet. I felt strong enough to swim to Mexico. This is where I would go to find my father and mother. I took another swallow of tequila.

Suddenly, I was ravenous, and the image of a fish roasting over coals became fixed in my mind. "A walleye!" I shouted at the masks.

But first I had to find a fishing pole.

I weaved between the junipers, over the crushed stones from the house to the road. I stumbled down the hill, my sandals slapping the asphalt and echoing against the low sky. I had begun to sweat, and my head felt as though it were stuffed with goose feathers.

I made it to the cement block boathouse, where I found an old spinning rig, with a dried worm still baiting the rusty hook.

The muddy brown surface of the lake bulged, rising and falling as though the currents were coming up to breathe. If I set out now on this swollen sea, the currents would pull me under in an instant, I thought.

I dug for a fresh worm with my hands, and with shaking, numb fingers tried to thread it onto the hook. I pricked my fingers twice before stitching the squirming animal into place. Watching the bait swirl through the sky as I cast made me dizzy. I nudged together two rocks to hold the rod. I couldn't wait to bathe, to let the water clear my head, which seemed less and less capable of directing the rest of my body.

I felt nothing except a brief stab in my groin when I waded naked into the lake. I splashed water over my face, arms, and chest and rubbed my skin with silt, working up a muddy slurry. Then I dove toward the bottom and pulled myself along the soft floor of the lake with my hands, my eyes open. Are you down here? I asked the stranger. Did you follow me? Or are the currents rolling you around the bottom of the lake?

I burst to the surface, gasping, out of breath. A sharp cold split through my head. My arms had turned into a blotch of blue and white. I was turning into wood.

My body quaked and my legs went into a spasm. Mist separated and lifted from the surface of the water. Among the shapes of the low clouds I saw a distant shore and a path breaching a bank. This would lead south to the mountainous desert plain of the Sierra

Madre Occidental, the homeland of my father. I would float on my back and kick my feet and let the clouds guide me across the lake.

A splash echoed. The tip of the fishing rod dipped and jerked. A fish. I plowed through the water to grab the rod's foam handle before it was dragged into the lake. When I bent down to pick up the rod, blackness and then bright colors pulsed before me. My fingers were too numb to operate the reel, so I walked up the grassy slope until my catch, a small walleye, flopped ashore. I hooked my stiff fingers into its gills. In my other hand I carried my shorts. Midway up the street toward the Mask House, my stomach convulsed. I stumbled and tripped. Pebbles and stones cut into my palms. The walleye slipped from my fingers. The tequila was poison after all! The masks had tricked me into drinking it! This was how they had planned to kill me: make me kill myself!

My wrist throbbed. Was it broken? Sweat covered my forehead. I tried to stand and walk, but dizziness hit me. I retched. The poison burned my throat as it came out, and I spoke the language of the ancestors, the words that I was supposed to say when Otis died but didn't. And then it was over. I heard water bubbling uphill of me and followed the sound. From a split in the asphalt, water gurgled into the street. Perhaps it was from a ruptured pipe, but it was clear and clean.

I crouched on the wet pavement and slurped water from the accidental spring and then stretched out below the little flow so the water could cleanse me.

What a fool. How could I have believed I'd be spared the masks' evil? That it existed for others and not for me? They'd been laughing at me the whole time as they lured me into their trap of the tequila. I'd only survived them, and the currents, too, because the singing wolves were stronger than any of this evil. The singing wolves were my guardian spirit. That was the revelation of my dream, I'm sure.

I didn't return to the house of the masks. Higher ground had always offered safety, and this was where I headed. At the top of the hill, the street joined a dirt road that led to a narrow, stone passageway overgrown with rows of Russian olives on each side. I almost didn't see it. The path opened upon first a shed, then a patio covered with a willow trellis, then a stone stove, and then a house. Beyond the house were an old orchard and a garden with a fence around it. The prairie started after this and stretched until it met the gray sky.

The house was tall, with a front door and windows that rose above a stone foundation partially hidden by June berry bushes. A wide porch wrapped from the front to one side. Peeling white paint covered its wooden sides. The front door was unlocked, but after I entered the house, I turned a knob until the lock clicked—added protection against the masks' evil.

I wandered through the ground floor of the abandoned house and ran my hands over the old furniture, touched the soft wool of the big chairs and drew my fingers through the dust on the round oak table. I didn't feel alone. People frozen in black-and-white photographs on the walls looked down at me: women and men with arms around waists or over shoulders, laughing as their dogs sniffed, fought, and humped each other. In the backgrounds of the photos, I could see the porch and garden, a table arranged with platters of food, a fire pit in a field, the deck of a sailboat in mid-lake, where naked people hugged and kissed and drank from tall brown bottles. These people filled the room with life, and I was sorry to have arrived too late to be in the photographs with them.

I settled into a large, dark-green chair and wrapped myself in a blanket made from wool all the colors of the rainbow. A wide stool, of the same dark-green fabric as the chair, gave my bowed legs plenty of room to rest. I slept through the afternoon and into the night. In the morning, I savored the drowsy feeling that sleep had brought. Brightness filled the room, the rain had stopped, the sun was out. I had a headache.

Later that morning, outside on the patio, under the willow trellis, I was overcome with a longing for the stranger's voice. For a moment, I believed that if I stood there long enough, someone would arrive to replace the memory of his speech. I couldn't move. I stood for minutes, listening for footsteps, words, a human's voice, but all I heard was the emptiness of the prairie ringing in my ears.

I collected my pack from the damp sand of the burned land behind the house. In the street I found the walleye, stiff and bent into a "J." I threw it into a ditch and then headed uphill, my pack slung over my shoulder.

I benefited from what the owners of the house had left behind. Upstairs in a bedroom off the end of the hall I found dry, almost new, clothes in a dresser: a pair of stretchy black underwear that fit me snugly, an orange shirt with buttons down the front, and a pair of dark-red pants that were baggy around the hips and wide and loose in the legs.

When I stepped back to see myself in the mirror hanging over the dresser, the first intact mirror I had ever seen, my sunken cheeks and dirty face, not my new clothes, caught my attention. "I'm a poor farmer from the Sierra Madre Occidental," I said to my reflection, although I looked much more beaten down than the farmers in the photographs in the blue booklet. I needed to eat.

I collected what I could around the house: chokecherries growing on the trellis; June berries along the foundation; a tangle of bean and pea vines, large fibrous zucchinis, dense hedges of spinach, spindly, pockmarked lettuce, and cloves of garlic and onion bulbs in the garden; and plums in a small orchard grove on the edge of the prairie.

On the patio I ate from a bright red plate that I imagined the people in the photographs had eaten off of as they sat around the rusting table, whose top was a design of flowers and leaves. The metal chairs were uncomfortable and hurt my back; I often ate standing up. As I shoveled food into my mouth, I imagined conversations and laughter, like the ones I thought the men and women in the photographs would have had. I wished that those people could have stepped out of their photographs and come onto the patio and told me what had happened to them, to this place.

Especially, I would have liked to talk to the two women in the large color photograph over the fireplace. The frame was painted gold, with vines carved into the wood. The women stood naked with a dog in the middle of the stone path. Their hands were on their hips and their feet were spread. The woman on the left had wavy, silver hair, full breasts, a round belly, and plump thighs. She wasn't smiling. The woman on the right had short, straight orange hair, small, taut breasts, a concave stomach, and skinny legs. She looked young enough to be the other woman's daughter. Her red lips were parted in a wide grin. The large thin dog with short wiry gray hair stood in front of them, its long wispy muzzle reaching just above the black triangles of the women's groins. "First and Last Family Portrait on the Eve of Goodbye, Parshall Bay" was written in pencil below the photograph. The laughing people in the black-and-white photographs had to have been their friends. Who had been killed, relocated? Who had run away or was searching for someone who had disappeared?

I tried to imagine the shutting down of this small community on Parshall Bay, the inevitable food and water shortages, the lack of electricity, the exit and disappearance of people. In White Earth River I had experienced this from my mother's breast, from my father's and Otis's arms, too young to remember except through Otis's stories, but a participant nonetheless. Separation or disappearance isn't the same as dying. In some ways dying is better because at least you know where the dead go—into the spirit world, where you have the chance of someday reuniting with them.

Before I could head south, I needed to harvest and dry the corn, secure seeds, and cure fish for the trip. I began to worry about finding the sail.

I tried to scavenge a sail and mast from one of the beached sailboats, but they were too large for the canoe. If the sailboats hadn't been so heavy, with their keels wedged into the slit, I would've dragged one to water's edge and launched it.

I scouted the shoreline for the sail, first on foot and then from the canoe. It was tedious work. I ran aground in muck when mats of reeds and driftwood tricked me into believing I had sighted the sail. The wide northern finger of the lake ended in a wetland that spread out over a kilometer before hitting dry ground. Lots of ducks, but no sail.

Eventually, I found it on the shoreline south of Parshall Bay. The wind had blown it into a shallow cove where it floated in ankle-deep water, rising and falling as though the white cloth were breathing. The mast and boom, partially buried in silt, had kept the sail anchored. I didn't want to believe that my search had ended, but the sail was there, dirty and wet, impossible to ignore. I couldn't pretend that I hadn't found it and stay up the hill in the women's house with the soft chairs and wide bed. There wasn't enough food to eat. And I hated being in a place haunted by people who had been there not so long ago. As I rinsed the mud off the fabric and checked it for tears, a wave of anger washed over me and I almost drew my knife to slice the sail into shreds. When the anger passed, sadness filled me, and I wanted to cry.

PART V: NOLA

When I set out from Parshall Bay, I sensed the route the stranger and I had taken down the lake. It was preserved just under the surface of the water and sloshed against the hull of the canoe to help me keep a straight navigational line. The afternoons of sailing alone had revealed this aspect of the lake, which is why I could always find my way back to White Earth Bay, no matter how far from shore I sailed or how near dusk I returned to the bay.

The day was sunny, and the gentle breeze allowed me to manage the sail while using a paddle to steer without a struggle. I scanned the southern shore of the Van Hook Arm for the path I had seen while drunk on the tequila but saw only a dense continuous band of trees. Perhaps I wasn't looking in the right place. I was sure there was a passageway south from the lake.

I paddled through the narrow bend of the lake and hoisted the sail to glide under the suspension of the bridge and into open water. This is when I saw Nola, not too far from the distant northern shore. The sun caught her boat, which sat low in the water. At first I couldn't tell whether she was man or woman. I saw only her boat and the long oars slicing the air. I couldn't believe my eyes.

Another person right there, one long tack away. Or was I imagining this? Had spending so much time in the house with photographs on the wall made me conjure up a person to fill my life? Although my time with the stranger hadn't gone well—and I had no guarantee that Nola wouldn't present another disaster—I didn't think about the outcome, only about the unlikelihood of meeting another person anytime soon. The inhabitants of Parshall Bay had vanished, but here, right before my eyes, was a person, another chance. I had to sail fast enough to cut off whoever it was and not let him or her get away.

Because the rudder was broken, I tied the mast line around my waist and used both hands to steer with the paddle as the wind set the boat on edge. When I was within a short paddling distance of Nola, I dropped the sail and drifted.

She seemed to be floundering, rotating in a circle, going nowhere. She'd dig the long oars of the boat into the water, but when she pulled on them, the starboard oar skipped over the surface while the port oar pivoted the craft unevenly. Her struggles made me wonder whether she knew how to row. Or perhaps she was in danger. How did she get here in the first place?

I paddled toward her. As I closed in, I could hear the oars straining in their oarlocks and churning up water and hitting against the hull. The boat was long and narrow and barely floated above the water line. Sunlight reflected off its purple hull. Aluminum outriggers mounted with oarlocks were suspended over the water. When Nola saw me, she dropped the oars and reached for a cylindrical object dangling from her chest and held it up. This was a monocular, I later learned. I continued to paddle toward her. When I was twenty or thirty meters away, she pulled another cylinder-shaped object—this time from her waist—and pointed it at me. She called out:

"Don't get any closer."

I backstroked to halt the canoe and sculled figure eights as I considered fleeing. What was she pointing at me? A laser capable of stunning me, she later explained.

What stopped me from leaving, though, wasn't fear of being stunned but her glow, which radiated like a halo against the dry landscape. If I hadn't heard the noise of her oars, I would've thought she was a mirage.

"I won't hurt you," I called out and waved.

She took up the monocular again. After a moment she clipped the laser onto her belt. The monocular swung from her neck. She grabbed the oars, satisfied, I guess, that I wasn't a threat.

"Who are you?" she shouted across the water.

"D. E.," I shouted back. "During-the-Event Pérez."

She didn't introduce herself but asked, "Where are you going?"

"Home."

"Where's that?"

"White Earth River."

"Is anyone there?"

"No. Just me. My grandfather died. And so did the stranger."

She drifted to within a few meters of me. She feathered her oars to turn her boat broadside and kept an oar and outrigger between us. I couldn't see her eyes because they were covered by black sunglasses but did have a good view of her skin. It was covered in sweat. Perhaps that's what made its golden color glow—sunlight reflecting off beads of moisture. She had well-developed arms and broad shoulders and practically no hair, only a stubble of yellow fuzz. She wasn't wearing a life preserver but a radiant purple sleeveless top that matched the color of the boat. She seemed not to have any fat on her body, only muscle, which bulged through her tight purple top and black shorts, and two prominent points on her chest—her nipples.

She had to be from the Center. No one living off the land or wandering and lost, like the stranger had been, could look this neat and clean. Someone with such perfect proportions and coloration and as thin as the boat she rowed couldn't be violent, I thought. Perhaps she was the perfect type of woman the stranger had wanted to find. But, still, how did she get here?

"Your grandfather? A disease?" she asked.

"No, old age," I said.

"And the stranger . . . what about him?" she asked.

"He ran away from a quarry," I said.

"A runaway, okay. But he died, you said."

"In the storm. Our boat capsized. He couldn't swim. I tried to save him, but the currents pulled him under."

"There're no currents, here. This is a reservoir. The only things in it are tree stumps and rocks, maybe a few junked cars."

"The Missouri River. It's down there. I felt it. The singing wolves protected me from it."

"Technically, you're correct. The Missouri runs through the lake, but the Garrison dam controls everything. That's why the water level rises and falls, discounting flash floods and evaporation. That's about the extent of the current, okay? A *vestige*. And wolves howl, they don't sing."

I didn't want to argue with her, although I started to doubt whether I wanted to waste much effort in convincing her to come back to White Earth River with me.

"No diseases, you're sure?"

"No diseases."

"Okay, then with the runaway dead, that gives me rights of first contact. You agree?"

"I guess so."

I didn't know what she was talking about, "rights of first contact."

"Of course, it would've been more interesting if I'd been *literally* the first to meet you, but since the runaway's dead that's irrelevant. *Officially*, I'd be considered the first."

"Uh-huh," I said.

What did it matter? Behind the aggression and impatience, her words hid something else, fear perhaps, or exhaustion?

She reached under her seat and retrieved a bottle and sucked from it. She wiped her lips with the back of her hand and rubbed a coating of sweat from her scalp.

"This energy drink is barely keeping me alive," she said. "I hope you have something better to eat in White Earth River."

I told her about the garden and how we could harvest vegetables, maybe catch a fish or goose, perhaps a deer.

"I would love some corn," she said. "We eat that in the Center."

"Yeah, we do, too."

"We?"

"My grandfather and I."

"I thought he was dead."

"He is. I mean before, after last year's harvest."

"Oh, right."

We drifted, not speaking, while the wind gently pushed us toward shore. The space between us gradually closed. Nola took a black square off her belt and spoke to it and then stared at it for a while.

"It's not far, the bay and your river," she said.

"I know. Did your thing tell you that?" I asked.

"My hedgehog? Yeah, its GPS. You know what that is?"

"No."

"It's a satellite-based navigation system. It generates maps and has a route and distance calculator. It also connects me to my parents and advisor, so I'm never by myself."

"It does everything," I laughed. I didn't believe her.

"As long as the sun can charge it."

She clipped the hedgehog back on her belt.

"By the way, I'm Nola," she said. "I guess you should know that if we're going to row together."

"No-la," I said her name slowly, weighting the *o* and *a*, as though the name were two words. "No-la."

"That's right. Nola. I'm from the Center."

"I figured you were."

"Good. Good."

She wanted me to lead; she'd feel safer that way, she said. But I told her that I'd paddle more slowly than she could row because I had only one paddle whereas she had two oars.

"Barely two oars," she said. "The starboard pin just cracked. I heard it. Now I have to nurse it or it'll sheer completely."

"We have rowboats. Maybe you can use one of their oarlocks."

"Does my boat look like a rowboat? This is a flat-water shell. The parts are performance titanium and carbon fiber with tight clearances. I'm sure what's lying around your place is old aluminum. I doubt it would fit."

"I have tools."

"Well, maybe we can fashion something. Worse case, I call for a part. But I'll get points deducted for lack of resourcefulness. I'd like to avoid that if I can."

I imagined a helicopter dropping a piece of metal from the sky and supposed it could drop food, too, if she asked for it.

Before we set off, Nola warned, "Remember, I have protection. If I fire this thing, the military will be here in five minutes." She patted the cylinder clipped on her belt.

I decided, then, that maybe her laser was more of a signal than a device that would stun me. I could cover a lot of distance in five minutes. I wasn't worried.

I wondered if Nola was the type of woman Otis had in mind for me, if his spirit or perhaps the singing wolves had delivered her to me. Yet, she didn't seem to be very friendly, and I worried that the conditions of companionship weren't going to be much different from those that the stranger had demanded: food, shelter, and some odd form of friendship.

The fractured oarlock made Nola's strokes unequal, and we paddled and rowed up the White Earth Bay in a crooked line. I put up with the slowness for a while but then suggested tying the boats stern to bow so Nola could concentrate on rowing with one oar while I paddled and steered us from behind. She agreed to try this arrangement. My bowline to her stern haul loop wasn't a secure connection. The yellow rope squeaked as the knot tightened under the strain of our uncoordinated movement.

As we entered the mouth of the muddy White Earth River, I relished the feeling of coming home. The stranger, despite his pleas for help, had been an intruder. But Nola, what was she? Did she want only food and help fixing her boat, or was she also forcing her way into my life? Or had I invited her to enter it? Was the pleasure of watching her glowing skin so powerful that I'd give up my plans to travel to the Sierra Madre Occidental? The more I thought about this, the more I thought I'd need to discourage Nola from staying very long. I didn't want my goal of finding my parents disrupted, as it had been with the stranger.

The late afternoon sun angled into the buttes east of us and revealed the eroded layers of light-brown, gray, and yellow sandstone and the dark folds of these formations, which were dotted with green circles of vegetation. These, too, gave me pleasure to watch.

The bends in the river required that I pay attention so we'd stay in the main channel. I tried to synchronize my strokes with Nola's, but our rhythm was inconsistent. We lurched back and forth, the tail and nose of our boats bumping into each other. Over the sound of her oar splashing water—she was a noisier rower than I was a paddler—she began to tell me how she was rowing around Lake Sakakawea for "thesis."

I asked her what this meant.

"Thesis is a type of experience," she started. "It's kind of like a test, but more than that. You study something and then write a report. Every senior has to do it. Some do lab studies, others do book research, and then some of us are allowed to go outside the Center for a field experience. I have a friend who's at a clothes-manufacturing facility that's sewing her designs based on this cool textile made of bamboo fiber. Because I'm athletic and sort of interested in science, they accepted my proposal to row around the perimeter of Lake Sakakawea and test a new sports nutrition formula. It would have a lot of applications. Military patrols, long-distance truck routes, field explorations. A proven drink would make everyone's work more efficient. I'm the guinea pig in the trials."

"A formula, you mean arithmetic?"

"Yeah, someone calculated it in the lab. I'm just testing the product. Mix the powder with water, guzzle it down, record the variables."

"That's what's in the bottle?"

"Right. It's an orange color, a little sweet, a constant energy source, but not very satisfying. It gives me loose stools."

"Your shit, you mean?"

"Yeah, kind of loose. Lack of fiber, probably."

Nola's oarlock, the working one, squeaked and filled the air. Her fragile boat seemed only sturdy enough for a day's outing.

"Did you row through the storm?" I asked.

"Took the day off," she said. "Rested in an abandoned house. Slept in a bed."

"I slept in a bed, too, a wide one, in Parshall Bay."

"All beds are wide, designed for two to four people . . . I'll have to pass thesis if I want to be selected for a Diversity Team."

"The stranger liked teams, too."

"This isn't a sports or production team, but a special one. You get to travel, not just around Lake Sakakawea like I'm doing, but on expeditions deep into the interior to make contact with other people. To check their genome."

"You mean people like me?"

"No, Pockets, intact breeding populations in remote settlements. You're just Overlooked, someone the government missed when they emptied out this area years ago. The reproductive program hasn't gone as well as the government had hoped. They cut the margins too close when they thinned out the continent to fit what they thought was the correct population-to-resource carrying capacity. It's always best to have a surplus, my father says, whether it's wealth, education, intelligence, people, land. You always need more than you think you do. People always miscalculate, make mistakes."

A surplus was certainly preferable for harvests, I thought.

"Now the population is starting to crash. We need more people. Diversity. Former Mexico. That's where we'd search first. Relocation and culling were pretty haphazard down there," Nola said.

"My father was from Mexico," I said.

"Was he a horticulturalist? Mexico had this massive seed bank. That's one reason we wanted them to be part of the continental government."

"He brewed *tesgüino*."

"That's a . . . ?"

"From corn. Not like tequila."

"You know about tequila?"

"I've had it."

"What's it like?"

"Smokey, warm. Everything seems alive, until the poison hits you."

"It's not allowed in the Center. No alcohol is. We have pills instead."

"It helped me see some things. I might drink it again."

"You have some?"

"No, in Parshall Bay. The masks are guarding it."

"Masks?"

"On the wall. The tequila is in a cabinet."

"Are you talking about artwork, maybe, sculpture, something someone collected?"

"I don't know. The masks are very old. And tricky. You have to watch out."

"Oh."

Nola frowned but didn't say anything. She concentrated on pulling her oar through the greenish-brown water as we made our way around a silent, gentle bend.

I began to worry that White Earth River might have changed while I was away, and as we rounded Goose Peninsula, I looked for signs of this. The nesting females called out their usual threatening welcome. The drab, gray boathouse on its short pilings, the shaky ramp leading to the dock, and the three half-submerged rowboats were as I had left them, although they seemed more weathered than they had before. Nola bumped her rowing shell against the dock. Because it didn't have a tether line, only a haul loop at the bow, she steadied it by holding onto one of the pitted dock cleats. I tied up the canoe with a section of the yellow rope and then cut another section to secure her boat.

"This is it, I guess, huh?" she said. She climbed onto the dock and stood to survey the boathouse, the beach, and the playing field. She pushed her sunglasses onto her head. One eye was blue, the other, green. That was why she wore the black lenses—to hide her mismatched eyes. She was a good head length taller than me.

"This part of town wasn't destroyed," I said.

Nola frowned and sniffed the air. Geese clucked in the playing field as they searched for insects and seeds and munched on grass and weeds.

"What stinks? The geese? Or maybe the water's fetid," she said.

"It's probably the boathouse. The stranger vomited inside," I said.

"I thought you said there were no diseases."

"The stranger was only sick in the boathouse. One night. Then I took him away. You don't have to go inside. The rest of the town is okay. And I'm healthy."

"You better be. I can't risk illness."

The sight of the geese made me hungry. The thought of their oily meat overpowered my desire to reassure Nola. But it seemed too near dusk to begin what I feared might be for Nola, as it had been for the stranger, an unpleasant experience, even if I used the netting to capture a goose. So I proposed catching fish.

"You'll have to teach me," Nola said.

"It's easy. We can cast from shore."

I had left the doors of the boathouse open, but still I feared the germs left behind in the stranger's dried vomit. I sloshed a bucket of water over the floor and swept the dirty water out the back door with a plastic broom. The sound of the water dribbling into the river worried me, and I hoped that any bacteria would wash downriver and into the lake.

I dug worms in the playing field and baited the hooks. Nola's casts were natural, fluid and silent. Unlike the stranger, she released the line on the spinning reel at just the right moment and hit the center of the river with each cast. She seemed to enjoy reeling in her first walleye, but I was the one to unhook it and whack its head against the ground, which didn't bother her. Perhaps she didn't understand I was killing it, or maybe she knew that this was necessary for us to eat. The fish in the Center came from fish farms, she said, not lakes or rivers. Their flesh was white, but she didn't know if they were walleye.

I showed her how to thread a worm onto a hook, which didn't bother her, either, and then while she fished I built a fire on the beach. I heard a fish splashing in the shallows and saw Nola take it off the hook and hold it by the tail and thwack it against the silt.

"Hey, During-the-Event, how many fish do we need?" she shouted up to me.

We already had three.

"We have time for a couple more. The fire has to burn down to coals," I said.

I couldn't believe how easily Nola had learned to fish and kill the catch, tasks that had filled the stranger with frustration and fear.

I went down to water's edge. Three more fish were lying in the silt. We were going to have a feast! I started to gut them and scrape the entrails into the water. Nola unclipped the black square from her waist, held it up to her mouth and spoke to it, and then pointed it at me.

"This is so primitive," she said. "And you're so dark in this light. I wish the fish bled more."

"What are you doing?" I asked, pointing my knife toward her black device.

"Just taking video. I'll show you later, if you want."

"Video?"

"Like photographs. Only moving. Like movies."

Otis had mentioned movies before, their stories, but not in association with devices.

"Oh."

"You don't mind, During-the-Event, do you? I guess I should've asked."

"No, it's okay. And you can call me D. E. My grandfather only called me During-the-Event when he talked about Hidatsa things."

"I like During-the-Event better. It's a man's name. D. E. is kind of sexless, childish."

"D. E. is what I'm used to."

"Letters. People talk in letters in the Center. I prefer real names. You become a human being with a name."

"Call me Pérez, then. That's my father's family name."

Her device beeped.

"Okay, Pérez, excuse me, I have to transmit. Only take a second."

She turned and walked down shore, her hedgehog held up to her ear so she could talk into it without my hearing her. I gathered the fish and took them to the fire. Was she mad? Had I angered her? She returned a few minutes later.

"Sorry. I have to stay in touch. My father's all for this, but my mother worries. I told them I was sleeping in a boathouse, my sleeping pad bolstered by a bed of life preservers. That seemed to make them happy."

I didn't tell her the stranger had done the same thing.

"I didn't mention the cracked oarlock, in case I need a day to fix it."

I placed the fish on the coals and turned them by their tails so they would cook evenly and not burn. When the skin began to bubble and pop, I arranged them on a rack of sticks to cool. Using my knife, I separated the moist flesh from the spine. We ate the pieces with our fingers.

Nola ate fast, faster than I did, and didn't speak as she chewed. There hadn't been much to eat in Parshall Bay, and I had had to rely on the MRGs in the house of the masks, where I found the tequila, but Nola devoured two fish in the time it took me to eat one.

"These are incredible," she said. "So different tasting than the ones we get in the Center and such a relief after the sports drink. It's not that I have a deficiency. My blood work is fine. I'm just hungry all the time."

"We can eat some vegetables in the garden, too. I need to check on them anyway. I've been away for a few days."

"I'm on my ninth day out and that includes a day off for the storm."

"How many more do you have?"

"Twenty in total. Fifty-five kilometers a day. I'm setting a record: first to row around Lake Sakakawea. But I've lost time because of the storm. And now the oarlock. I might have to put in some long days to catch up."

"Then you better eat another fish."

"Thanks, but you look like you could use another one, too. You're kind of scrawny."

The intense gaze of her blue and green eyes made me uncomfortable. I eyed the head and tail of the fish she had finished. A band of meat along the spine she had neglected. I chewed the head of my fish and thought about finishing the remains of hers. I didn't say anything.

"I mean, how old are you?" she asked.

"Not that old. Twenty-eight seasons plus a few years. We began to count the seasons sometime after I started walking and using tools."

"Then what, seventeen, eighteen?"

"Maybe. How old are you?"

"Eighteen."

She smiled and bobbed her head from side to side. Orange and blue stones hung from her ears on gold wires; they swung back and forth as she tilted her head.

"Your early development was probably off," she said and pointed a long, tapered finger at me. I could hear the material of her shorts rubbing as her legs moved against each other. I didn't know what she was talking about.

"I mean, food must've been hard to come by, huh?" she asked.

"My grandfather said it was, but I don't remember. I had my mother's milk until she died. Then he chewed food for me."

"So you could swallow it."

I had created images to match Otis's stories of my early life: wrapped tightly in a blanket, riding strapped against his back, or left napping in a hammock tied to thick trunks of cottonwoods while he worked in the garden or cut wood.

"I can tell you suffered by your legs and the fact that you're short for your age."

"The stranger thought my legs were deformed, too. He said I was pliered."

"Well, your legs are just fine, huh? They're not deformed, and I'm sure they're very strong. And you certainly weren't pliered, whatever that means."

"I never thought I was. That's just the way he talked when he was mad."

"Then you're lucky he drowned."

It wasn't luck, but I was afraid to mention the currents again. Or the singing wolves. I didn't want her to laugh at me.

"The reason your legs are bowed is when you lost your mom's milk, your body wasn't quite ready for the food your grandfather fed you. Rickets, that's what it's called. I bet there were other times when food was scarce, huh?"

Had it been the cool season when Otis thought about letting me starve? Without asking, I lifted one of the skeletons Nola hadn't eaten and sucked the meat off the spine. I described the times of near starvation in the cool season, when we ate the same mush of ground corn, sunflower seeds, and sometimes acorns and chewed the inner bark of box elders, and how our snares remained empty, the deer eluded capture, the geese flew away, and fish rested in the cold water at the bottom of the river, uninterested in our bait.

I found myself exaggerating our story of hardship, whereas in fact as Otis and I had become better gardeners and hunters, we suffered less, especially if the cool season was mild and the harvest had been plentiful.

Nola shifted in the sand and cooed in sympathy.

All this talk of starvation made me hungry, and I thought of the garden and how sweet the fresh corn was. I felt my mouth watering and licked back drool that was starting to form.

"You're probably teetering on the brink of a nutritional crisis, from the looks of you. You have no reserves. A bad week or two and you start to cannibalize muscle," she said.

I looked at her blankly.

"When you're not taking in enough food, your body begins to eat up your muscle. It's only a matter of time before you stop functioning."

"I feel okay."

"Maybe right now, but say you have a bad month. No fresh meat. Your immune system crashes, then it's too late. You get sick and die."

I wondered if that was beginning to happen when I drank the tequila.

"Let's go to the garden," I said. "There's fresh corn and carrots. First of the season. It's sweet."

"Sure, why not? What about the fire?"

"It's almost burned out."

"Let me get my kit. I'm beginning to feel chilled."

She fetched a small black bag from the bow of her boat and slung it over her shoulder.

"Lead the way," she said.

We walked along the beach and up the path toward the foot-bridge in the dark-gray light of dusk.

"You know, this place is kind of neglected," Nola said. "The sunken boats, the rotting boathouse, the unmown field. I'm surprised you've stayed."

"I was born here," I said. "There's the garden and plenty of game. We can scavenge clothes from the ruins. I learned to swim and paddle the canoe in the river."

"I don't think I'd swim in this water with all the goose shit . . . and the innards you dumped. Maybe it looks okay during the day, but right now it feels kind of hemmed in and menacing."

She pointed toward the rise of Windy Butte: "And that has a depressing quality."

I looked up at the rim of the butte. It was catching the last rays of sunlight. I liked this time of day, when the light was fading and the air was becoming cooler. Sunshine isn't a measure of a place, I thought. Even the ruins of the town looked cheerful on a sunny day.

My spirits dropped when I saw the rows of vegetables. Squash were rotting, lettuce lay wilted on the ground, leaves of tomato plants were riddled with holes, and the broccoli stalks were becoming as stout as small trees. Zucchini were as thick as pike. Deer had broken through the netting and ravished rows of the corn.

"Damn deer," I said.

"What greedy bastards," Nola said.

I appreciated her sympathy but doubted whether she understood the seriousness of the damage. I wanted to cry. All the work that had gone into the garden, not just this season but also all the seasons since I was old enough to help Otis, seemed on the verge of being lost. And it was my fault for leaving, for staying away so long. If I'd killed the stranger, gotten it over with quickly, life could've returned to normal. I wouldn't have been stuck in Parshall Bay looking for the sail. I wouldn't have wasted time meeting Nola. I wouldn't now be facing a possible cool season of scarcity.

Without speaking, I ripped an ear of corn from its stalk and pulled back the husk and devoured the ripe kernels. I savored their sugar. Nola stood by and watched. When I finished my ear, I snapped one off for her and showed her how to form a handle with the husk. She couldn't keep up with my pace of eating, though. I needed the corn as much as I had needed the fish. I stopped eating after the third ear. Nola had finished only one. I cleaned the stray kernels that she had missed on her ear and threw the cob into the dirt.

"I look forward all season to this, being able to eat corn in the fields. It's sweetest right after you pick it," I said.

"It doesn't need anything—butter, salt, pepper," she said.

"That's right, it's good by itself."

"Don't worry, we'll get that fucking deer."

"Do you sleep on the ground?" Nola asked after we had eaten two carrots. "I don't like to, but I can. I have a pad that makes it not so hard or cold."

"After my grandfather died I did, but then I moved into a mono-rail car. I cut sod for a bed and lined it with dried grass," I said.

"Is that where we'll sleep tonight?"

"No, we'll sleep in the cave. It has beds. Not wide ones. Only narrow ones."

"The cave?"

"Up there." I pointed to Windy Butte.

"I can't see it."

"No, not from here. You have to climb the butte. That's why we were never detected, even when people wandered through the valley."

"But now you're not hiding in the cave."

"No, now it's different, with my grandfather having died."

"Okay. But you're going to show it to me."

"Yeah."

We started up the grassy terrace. We bypassed the collapsed houses of the town, to the left, already hidden in the shadows that dark-ness had brought to the valley. I led her around outcrops and along dusty benches toward the upper slopes of Windy Butte, where the remains of sunlight, reflected by a few clouds, made it easier to see the path. Still, I avoided the steep slab, a route I was sure she could skip up during the day and perhaps even under a full moon, once she learned the way. She walked behind me, close enough to touch, and I wondered if she sensed the animal spirits nestled in the butte. Flat, dark-blue clouds rimmed in red filled the sky. I knew it would be sunny tomorrow.

I didn't want to reveal my worries about a snake having taken up residence in the cave. Otis and I always returned to the cave well before dark, and the one time we did find a snake—a bull snake, not poisonous—I killed it with a shovel. The meat tasted fine, but we didn't tan the skin correctly and it fell apart.

"I'm sorry," I said. "I don't have any candles. We'll have to go slowly. The back of the cave is very dark."

"Wait, I have a light."

She reached into her black bag and pulled out a flashlight. I took it from her and watched as its beam filled the entrance with blue light. I shined the light into the back corners of the cave, under the beds, and over the willow matting. The sight of everything—the furniture, stove, and shelves of dishes, books, and pots and pans—reminded me of what I had missed. I stepped inside the cave and ran my hands over the table to clear it of grit, to feel its familiar surface.

I motioned with the light for Nola to enter. She stooped and passed between the stove and the wall. When she stood up, her head nearly bumped against the ceiling. I turned the beam upwards and caught the drawings I had smeared in the soot on the cottonwood beams.

"Oh, those . . . my mother would love them," she said.

"I was young," I said.

"They're worthy of a museum."

I liked the way Nola's light sharpened the stick figures and animals. They weren't threatening like the masks on the wall of the house in Parshall Bay had been, but comforting, welcoming. I had made them one night during a cool season. While I had stood on a chair and smudged the drawings in the soot with my finger, Otis had simmered a rabbit in a broth of onions, garlic, and potatoes. He sang a song with English words: "If you remember me, I'll remember you, and the memory will pull us down the road." His English songs always sounded better than his Hidatsa songs, not only because I could understand the words but also because they had a melody that I could hum.

"And the furniture. It's so rustic. I love it," Nola said.

"My grandfather scavenged it, except for the beds. He made those with lumber from the Catholic church. He said it helped him remember his wife. She was Catholic. He wasn't."

"He was romantic."

"Hidatsa. That's the type of Indian that used to live here."

"Maybe that, too."

"He wasn't really Hidatsa, though. He just wanted to be. He wanted to go back to a time before all this, before there were white people."

"Hmm."

"I guess you can sleep here," I pointed to my bed. "The mattress isn't as comfortable as the ones in a house."

"You'll sleep with me, right?"

"I was going to sleep in my grandfather's bed."

"No, you don't understand. I never sleep by myself. As soon as I stopped sleeping with my parents, I started sleeping with my cohort. That's why thesis is so hard. Sleeping alone in abandoned houses or in the dark on the muddy shore is more difficult than rowing all day."

"There's probably not enough room for both of us."

"Sure there is," she said. "I'm not fat."

She set her flashlight on the wooden stand between the beds and peeled off her purple rowing top. Small pale breasts sprang forth and caught the blue light reflecting off the cave wall. She turned toward me, as if to point her two hard brown nipples at me. Her breasts had been flatter and firmer, hidden under the purple top, and now they looked out of place against her dark chest. She worked off her pants and kicked them across the room. Her groin and buttocks caught the light, too. Without clothes, she seemed to move in a different way, as though she had one body in her rowing clothes and another when she took them off. Her buttocks shook, for one thing, and she rounded her shoulders and caved in her chest, for another, as though she were cold from the dampness in the cave.

"You've probably never seen a naked girl before, have you?" she asked.

She stood up straight and smiled, with her hands on her hips. Her white teeth beamed from her golden face.

"Just in the photographs at the house," I said.

"Yeah, but that doesn't count. Come on, take off your clothes. I'll give you a tour."

She sat on the edge of the bed and watched me slip off my shorts and pull my shirt over my head—I never bothered to un-button it. I let the clothes sit in a heap on the willow matting near my feet. My body had none of the pale areas that Nola's did, since I often didn't wear clothes in the middle of the day or when I was on the river.

"Come on, sit down beside me," she said.

The smell of her body was strong: sweat baked into her skin by the sun, the faint smell of fear, and a musty, woodsy odor that I'd never smelled before.

"OK, give me your hands," she said.

She took them into hers and breathed on them.

"They have to be warm for this. You ready?"

I laughed and said yes, wondering if she were about to tell a joke. She placed the palms of my hands over her breasts.

"You can't feel much when you touch me this way, can you?"

"No."

And it was true. The weight of my hands squished her breasts into her chest.

"You have to do it like this."

She moved my fingers across her nipples.

"Lightly," she said, "squeeze them, but not too hard. That's right. Keep doing that . . . and you can . . ."

I felt her nipples become taut. She turned and she kissed me on the lips. I tasted salt and the sourness of her fear. Her tongue began to swim around my tongue, along the insides of my cheeks, against the roof of my mouth. She held my face between her hands. She opened her mouth wider, like a fish, and pressed her lips hard against my mouth. She had a very long tongue. To keep my balance I held onto the thin mattress.

She stopped kissing and pulled back and breathed hard, catching her breath. She had a heavy look on her face, as though she were dazed or sleepy.

"I forgot to ask you," she said. "Did you sex with the stranger?"

"You mean drive the bone?" I asked.

"Is that what he called it?" She laughed. "Well, it doesn't matter. Boys sex with each other all the time. So do girls. We all have our own words for it."

"He offered to do me, but I told him I was saving myself for my wife."

"Oh, how romantic! So I really *am* the first."

"Yeah."

"Well, then. Do you know what a clitoris is?"

"No."

"What about a vagina?"

"No."

"Okay, we'll start with the clitoris. It's sort of like a penis only a little smaller."

She lay back on the bed and spread her legs. She guided my hands to her groin, which was moist.

"There. You feel that?"

She had placed my finger on a firm little bump.

"You'll lick this with your tongue. Not for very long. Start gently and then build up pressure."

It seemed an odd thing to do, but I had enjoyed kissing her and liked her musky smell. So I did. I felt it grow in size and firmness as I licked it and Nola pushed my head into her groin. It was difficult to breathe, and with her thighs pressed against my ears, her groans were muffled. When she stopped and let go of my head, I rose up panting.

She grabbed my penis and licked the end of it. The warmth and wetness of her mouth made it swell to the size it sometimes reached in the middle of the night as I dreamed.

"Now, we're ready for the vagina."

She tapped my chest.

"Lie back," she said and then crawled on top of me.

She fumbled to get me inside her. Her opening wasn't as moist as her mouth. I felt pressure—she was moving around—then wetness and warmth.

"Oh!" she gasped. I smelled the fish on her breath.

"Are you okay?" I asked.

"Don't move, just stay still," she said.

She grabbed my wrists and held them against the bed next to my head. Her movement was slow and random at first, but when her blue and green eyes began to cross, it became a concentrated rhythm. She bore down on me and clutched my shoulders to help her slide faster. Then she started grunting.

"Come on, you move, too!" she shouted.

Her breasts quivered above me. The bed creaked and rocked as though it would split apart. I felt as though I were a plant buried in her ground.

My penis released deep inside of her. She mashed herself into me and collapsed, smothering me with her body. I held her tight, and she filled my ear with atonal sounds, ending with a long, high-pitched moan that faded into silence. She stayed on me, motionless, until I fell out of her, and then she rolled off and lay on her back, knees spread and bent, pointing toward the watermarks and mold on the ceiling. She fanned her stomach. I felt the breeze on my damp body.

"You were almost screaming. And the bed?" I said.

"I thought it was pretty good," she said. "For a first time."

"Yeah," I said.

I couldn't imagine Otis and Malèna coupling like this in the juniper. The branches couldn't tolerate such shaking and bouncing. Nor could I imagine that what we had just done was the same relaxing pastime that Otis had hinted making love was. I rested a hand on Nola's knee, and she scooted against me, her wet groin against my thigh.

"Look," I said, and pointed to my penis. "Is that from you?"

"That's nothing. A little blood. Forget it," she said and frowned. "You know, you're not very enthusiastic."

"Were we making love?"

"That's an old term. Sexing is the correct term. We were sexing on the frontier."

"Is it like this every time?"

She squeezed my belly and laughed.

"No. It's never the same. And it's best to forget your first experience as quickly as possible. Then you'll want to do it again. And the more you do it, the better you are, the more intense the sensation. You'll see. We're just getting started."

"My grandfather hinted at this, and it seemed to be the only thing the stranger wanted. But I wasn't sure what they were talking about."

"You would've figured it out sooner or later. You would've met someone."

"That's what my grandfather, thought, too. You do this every night?"

"Most nights, and sometimes during the day. It depends on who's around and if we have free time. Boys, girls, we like to do it together, huh?"

"You pick someone and just start doing it. That's what the stranger said."

"Both people must agree. . . . And think, if I'd been ovulating, I'd have gotten pregnant. My eggs, your sperm."

"My sperm?"

"What you left inside me. If my ovaries had released eggs, they'd be joined together by now."

"That's how it works?"

"When the lab isn't involved."

I had never considered how I came to exist. Otis had never talked about it or how other animals entered the world. Our focus had been on how long it took to kill animals once they'd been caught or trapped and then how to respect their spirits. That my parents had done this sexing, perhaps noisy with drink, seemed hard to believe. And Otis and Malèna entwined and making love, whether in a bed in Bismarck or in the sap of the juniper—it all seemed to be of another world.

"But I probably can't escape the lab," Nola said. "I'll have to be implanted with sperm not of my choice. That'll make it easier not to keep the result. Just another lab rat for the dorms."

Nola was silent for a moment then said, "Let's not talk about this anymore. Let's go to sleep."

She nuzzled against my shoulder, and with my free hand I pulled the frayed, patched cotton blanket over us and draped my arm around her. "You really melted me," she said. My body settled into the contours of the cornhusk mattress. A breeze barely made it to the back of the cave and stirred up the musky smell of our bodies. Nola jerked and twitched as she fell asleep. Our quiet lovemaking had let me ignore my memory about Otis's last day here at the back of the cave. I turned my head now, toward his bed. I could feel his spirit sitting on the edge of it and laughing.

I clutched the hem of the blanket against my neck but couldn't fall sleep. I wanted to get up and go to the garden and pick the corn. I wanted to install another rudder on the canoe and sail to the Sierra Madre Occidental. Now I understood what Otis meant when he used to tell me not to waste time.

Nola was naked, sitting at the table and looking at her hedgehog when I woke up. I hadn't heard her leave the bed. The soft morning light at the cave's entrance made her skin look different, less golden and shiny, more dusty and mottled. Her breasts had a different shape, too, softer, rounder, fuller. Freed from the tight purple top and perhaps having benefited from my touching them the night before, they had seemed to grow.

I pulled on my shorts and cinched tight the deerskin belt. I moved my June berry–stained chair around the table and set it next to her so our bare shoulders touched. She was sitting in Otis's chair. She smiled at me and held up her empty bottle to ask for water. I filled it with what remained in the inner tube bladder. From her bag she brought out a black pouch containing another device, which was about the length of her flashlight. She removed its plastic cover and inserted its clear rod into the bottle. The rod lit up as she stirred the water. "Just making sure it's safe," she said.

I told her that the water was clean, from the crack in the street in Parshall Bay, and that I hadn't gotten sick. "I have to treat all sources with suspicion if I want to stay healthy," she said.

When she was finished sterilizing the water, she added three envelopes of the powdered sports nutrition formula and shook the bottle. Then she drank without offering to share any with me.

"Ah," she said, after gulping down the contents of the bottle. "What a way to wake up. Now it's time to record some variables." She smiled, as though this was something I'd enjoy, too.

She pulled another small black device, a flat circular one, from her bag and set it on the table. She attached a round white patch to her chest and a plastic clamp to her finger. A graph with wavy red, blue, yellow, and green lines appeared on the screen of her hedgehog. The device beeped, and she tugged off the patch and clamp.

"No change yet. Maybe your food won't skew the findings after all. Now that would be something to explain!" She punched me lightly in the arm.

"It was good food," I said.

"Yeah, but I'm not supposed to be eating anything besides the formula."

"You can't live on that."

"If it's all you have . . ."

She let her voice trail off and smiled again, showing her white teeth.

"During-the-Event, I mean Pérez, have you ever had your blood tested?"

"No."

"Well, it's a beneficial test. It can tell you a lot about yourself, huh?"

"I already know most everything."

"I mean useful stuff, like your disease potential, where your family came from."

She reached for my hand and placed my finger on an impression in the black circular device.

"I know where my family came from," I said.

"Really?" she said, then, "You'll feel a moment of discomfort," as she held my finger down firmly on the pad. "Sample," she told the machine.

"My father's ancestors were from the Sierra Madre Occidental," I said.

I felt what was like a bee sting and tried to pull my finger away, but Nola kept pushing it down until she said, "End."

I sucked on my finger.

"The first time it hurts, huh? But you get used to it. I do mine every day. I won't know the results right away, though."

"I have a book. With pictures." I kept sucking my finger.

"From Mexico?"

"Yeah."

I got the blue booklet from my rucksack and opened it to the photograph of the man leading his mule to market.

"The pages are a little wrinkled," I said. "They got wet."

"Don't worry, I'll be careful," Nola said.

She thumbed through the pages and studied the photographs and maps.

"This is really old. Your grandfather gave it to you?"

"No, it fell off the shelf in the house with the masks."

"And you just picked it up?"

"Yeah."

She returned to the spread of photographs in the middle of the booklet.

"Well, in any case, you do have a slight resemblance . . . to the Tarahumara," she said. "But we'll see what the blood work says." Then she smiled and handed the booklet back to me. I felt embarrassed for having shown it to her.

She spoke to her hedgehog, and photographs of people appeared. Their skin varied in tone from very dark, almost black, to pale white, and the color and texture of their hair ranged from straight and yellow to fuzzy and black.

"My cohort," she said.

"Cohort?" I asked.

"Like a family. We've been together since the beginning, but I lived with my parents until I started school. I was lucky. Not everyone has parents. Some of the lab rats can only live in dormitories."

"Lab rats?"

"That's what we call ourselves. The Petri dish kids. Here they are. Mom and Dad. Hi, June. Hi, Henry."

"Can they hear you?"

"No, we're not connected."

Her parents were sitting at a white table, barely smiling. Her father had white hair and taut, smooth tan skin with no wrinkles. Her mother had the same type of skin but short, cropped black hair. Their eyes looked weary and old, like Otis's right before he died. Although the photographs were in color, her parents looked less alive than the farmers of the Sierra Madre Occidental or Otis and Malèna in their black-and-white photos.

"They're very old," I said.

"Sort of. They're probably in their late nineties, but they've been preserved to about age sixty. I think they regret not dying when they had the chance. My father's a history teacher. His favorite saying is 'The weight of history is oppressive.' He thinks that because

I'm an athlete, I'll be able to outrun history! That's one of his jokes. Whenever I'm in a competition, he says, 'Movement frees you from the weight of history.' He laughs every time he says it. He thinks he's being really funny, but actually he's only a little funny. Still, I love him. My mom's a painter. Or used to be. She's sad all the time, but doesn't want anyone to know it. She made me these earrings for my eighteenth birthday." Nola touched the blue and orange stones hanging from her ears. "Kind of a going-away present, huh?"

"Your mother looks really old."

"Well, she's not *really* my mother. Biologically, that is." Nola laughed. "I didn't happen that way. I mean, a long time ago she of course reproduced the old-fashioned way, but not for me."

"So then who's your mother?"

"She is! June. I was assigned to her. And Henry."

She sighed and then said very slowly: "The way it's done in the Center is sperm and eggs are joined in a Petri dish. Once the egg is fertilized, it's implanted in an eighteen-year-old's uterus. She experiences the pregnancy and delivers naturally. The baby becomes part of a new cohort and is raised in a dormitory, or like me, with a set of old parents."

"I was born in the upstairs bedroom, I think."

"I'm sure there wasn't a lab in your town."

"A clinic."

"Maybe a midwife, if your mother was lucky."

Otis never talked about how or where I entered the world, only that I existed. Nola's explanation of the lab technique didn't make much sense to me.

She spoke to her device again and several photographs sped across the screen of her with hair in different colors and lengths.

"There. That's me with black hair, like yours," she said.

"Oh, I like it like that. Long," I said.

"Well, enjoy the picture. It'll take a year or two for it to reach my shoulders. It'll be weeks before I have much more than this fuzz."

Otis and I had passed years together where nothing seemed to change, our age or height; even our hair didn't grow very fast.

"Hey, you want to know a secret?" Nola asked.

Her eyes brightened, and she leaned toward me, whispering. I smelled sweetness on her breath.

"It's my father's and mine. He told me because my mother gets upset if he tells her anything disturbing. I think it's okay if I tell you, since you're an Overlooked, and this is a story about another Overlooked.

"Two years ago my father was on a trip up north. It was an award for agreeing to keep on living? He wanted to go to Paris, but of course Europe was off-limits because we had cut off relations with them when the United States retreated from the world and set up the continental government. Who knows what was happening over there. So he settled on a kayaking trip. Armed agents guided the group. My father was the slowest, because he's not in shape like he was when he was young, and he slipped behind, out of sight around a bend. He saw a man on the shore, standing beside a bush. Tattered pants, not wearing a shirt. His chest was brown, his hair long, light from the sun, and all matted together. My father made eye contact with him. His eyes were blue, both of them. He was maybe ten meters away. The agents had warned them of Pockets. As my father started to drift past him, he turned, to make sure that the guy was still there. He looked so lonely, standing by himself, that my father waved to him. But the guy didn't wave back. There was some turbulence my dad had to paddle through, then when he looked back again, the guy was gone.

"Isn't that a sad story?"

She sounded as though she might cry.

"Maybe he was going to fish or swim or just wanted to look at the river," I said. I wanted her to be happy. "He probably wasn't alone. I'll bet he had a family, a grandfather, or a father."

"No, he was alone. My father could see his ribs. He was going to die. This was the most authentic moment my father ever had, and I'm the only one he can share it with. If he'd told the agents, they probably would've shot the guy. Just for fun. So they could brag about killing an Overlooked."

Her voice cracked. She spoke to her hedgehog in a clipped whisper and the photographs disappeared. The screen went blank.

I thought of the word Nola used to describe me. Overlooked. Would Otis have laughed at that? Been insulted? Embraced it? The Overlooked, a tribe of two. Probably, he would have thought that we didn't need that name, Overlooked, because he had adopted Hidatsa for us. I wasn't like the man in Nola's story, hungry and alone along a river. Maybe having lived with one person made the difference between being Overlooked and being something else, a gardener and trapper, a survivor.

Nola continued to sit at the table and stare at the blank screen of her hedgehog, as though she couldn't decide whether to turn it back on. Perhaps she had forgotten to record something. Perhaps the device needed charging in the sun. Perhaps she was weighing trying to fix her boat or call for a new part. Perhaps she wanted to drink more formula. I had no idea. When I asked if her advisor had told her to row back to the lake and get back on route, she made a gruff "humph" sound, as Otis had sometime done, and said, "I'm on thesis. I'm the one who decides what I do."

Okay, I thought, and put on my shirt and sandals. I told her that I needed something to eat. Then what she said next surprised me. "What about the deer?" she asked.

"I'll have to repair the fence," I said.

"The one who ate the corn, though, don't you have to kill it?"

"I don't know which one ate the corn. They all do that, if they can."

"But living here you'd know the specific one? Haven't you identified him?"

"No. One might break the fence one time, then another, another time. And any deer eats what's easiest to eat."

"Then really you have to punish all of them."

She sounded disappointed, and I didn't understand why she had elevated a random nuisance, a chance opportunity for the deer, to an intentional violation of some rule. I focused instead on her enthusiasm for killing a deer and her strength and endurance and coordination and patience. She didn't seem to have any fear.

"My grandfather and I always trap a deer at harvest time," I said.

"Yeah, we won't let them get away with it," she said.

"We'll need to set a section of net in the forest, on the edge of a meadow, and chase one into it," I said, already visualizing our stalking.

"I'm a fast sprinter."

"They're not around, now. Later in the afternoon when it starts to cool and the sun lowers."

"I can fix my boat in the meantime."

"I could teach you how to pick corn."

"That sounds kind of tedious. But maybe for a little while."

"I'll give you some clothes to wear. So yours don't get dirty."

I rummaged in the dresser for a pair of Otis's shorts and a shirt, ones that he hadn't worn since the previous warm season.

"Mr. Peter James, he was too old to run from the machines. That's what my grandfather said. His ribs came apart when I tugged off this shirt." I handed the shirt to her. "I put his bones in a canvas bag and took them up to the cemetery. They knocked together and made a hollow sound as I walked. My grandfather always insisted we bury any bones we found, even if they weren't complete skeletons."

Nola stared at me as she accepted the shirt and shorts. Without a word she changed into them and stuffed her rowing clothes and her devices in the black bag. As we hiked down the slab of the Windy Butte, I was pleased that its steepness didn't scare her.

I showed Nola how to pluck corn with a sharp downward snap. She imitated my motion, but relied on endurance to compensate for crude technique. When her wrists and hands became sore from the work, I let her use my knife to cut the corn from the tall stalks. Meanwhile, I mended the fence.

As morning passed and the sun bore down on us, Nola took off her shirt. So her skin wouldn't burn, she asked me to rub a white cream from a small tube over the soft stubble of her head and her back, arms, and chest, with a particular emphasis on her pale breasts. Massaging the oily lotion into them led to sex, and I was pleased that Nola liked it as much as I did, standing in the rows of corn with Otis's shorts lying on the ground by her dirty feet.

In the afternoon we retreated to the bench in the cottonwood grove, where I showed her how to braid ears of corn into long strands that I draped to dry over willow rods supported by forked elm posts. Nola began to lag and complained of a headache and held out her hands to show me the cuts and blisters. Her palms were stained brown from grime and the juice of the cornstalks.

"I'm getting heat stroke," she said. "Usually by this time of day I've jumped into the lake a few times to cool off."

"Make sure you drink a lot of water."

"I don't like the taste. The smell, either. Not even the powder disguises it."

"I'll make you some tea. The water tastes better once it's boiled."

I told her where to find Otis's hat and the pot and two mugs in the cave.

"You remember the way up the butte?" I asked.

"Can you go, Pérez?" she asked. "I'm feeling nauseous. Headaches always make me feel sick to my stomach."

I liked that she had stopped using During-the-Event and called me by my father's family name.

"Sure. But stay in the shade," I said and pointed to the bench.

I started off in a jog. Where could I find a patch of ground cherry to brew for her? Honey would make the tea taste better. Otis added it to hot water along with butterfly weed root to soothe sore throats and coughs. Maybe I could melt some of the comb for Nola's hands. Deer fat would be good for her sore and dry hands, too.

Nola woke up when I set Otis's hat over her face.

"The leaves." She motioned toward the branches of the cotton-woods. "They put me to sleep." She sounded as though she were still in a dream.

"They do that to me, too. Keep sleeping if you want. I'm going to find some ground cherry and honey."

"Be careful, Pérez, don't get stung."

I laughed to myself over the sound of my father's name. It made me happy to hear it. I headed off toward the monorail car, following worn deer trails down the valley, through meadows and past clumps of willows and Russian olives until I found ground cherry. The yellow-green flowers were nodding toward the ground, and the lance-shaped leaves stood out against the surrounding grasses.

Across the river were a field and woods that spread up a slope. Deer often passed through the meadow and grazed on the grass and buds and flowers. If we could hang nets in the trees, we might be able to chase a yearling into them. I had killed a deer by myself only a few times. It was easier to do with two people. And I didn't want to celebrate the harvest without venison.

Otis had always been the one to remove the covers from our four hives and brush the bees off the frames in the supers. Most of the time he'd managed not to be stung, while I had watched from a safe distance. We would wait for calm, dry conditions, later in the day when the temperature had gone down so the bees would be less aggravated.

As I lifted a wooden cover, I remembered Otis's quiet but quick movements amid the humming and vibrating and tried to breathe slowly and evenly. I held a frame over the white plastic pail and cut out the comb. It was thin and waxy but would taste sweet nonetheless. I didn't want to take the time to scrape off the caps and drain the comb. Bees circled around me and flew up against my face. The ones that had fallen to the ground crawled onto my feet. I didn't try to brush them away or swat at them, and eventually they left me alone. I placed the cover back on the hive and tied a torn square of nylon around the pail's opening. This is how Otis had done it.

Nola had dragged driftwood from the riverbank. She was wearing Otis's old straw cowboy hat tilted back on her head. It was stained with Otis's sweat, the brim crinkled and bent, the black headband dusty and gray.

"I'm gathering kindling, Pérez. Isn't that what you need for a fire?"

"Yeah."

I laughed out loud this time when I heard my father's name.

"You're feeling okay, now?" I asked.

"Much better. I just needed a nap, that's all. Headache's almost gone, but I'm still looking forward to that tea you promised."

I built a fire over the charred remains of the ones I had made while living in the monorail car and boiled the root of the ground cherry until the water turned light brown. While the pot cooled, I stirred in a big spoonful of honey and comb, tasted the tea for sweetness, and added another one.

"You're going to like this, I know," I said.

I poured Nola a mug, and she took a long sip.

"It's a different kind of sweet from the powder, and I can taste a sharpness underneath," she said.

"That's the ground cherry."

"It stays in your throat."

"Honey's good for sore throat, too."

"Thanks, Pérez. I was really starting to fade."

"But you're okay now."

"Yeah, fine, don't worry. I have a second wind."

"Then you're ready for a deer? There'll be a lot of them soon, in the meadow, when the light fades."

"I've been waiting all day for that."

"Good."

As we drank the tea, I explained how we would tie the fine black netting onto lengths of cottonwood and hang them on branches so the deer would become entangled in the mesh when we chased them toward the woods. I would set bait—ears of corn on sticks. We would have to wait, maybe a long time, and maybe we wouldn't catch one. Maybe we'd end up eating only corn and greens.

"Sometimes you can get close to them," I said. "The trick is not to scare them until you're ready to charge. You have only one chance. You have to be certain. Otis and I have tried everything."

"Otis?"

"My grandfather."

"You use his first name? That's really funny. We're the same, you and me, calling our parents by their first names."

"It's what his workers called him. Like the elevator. When he did iron work in the Center."

"That's so funny."

I resumed telling Nola about trapping a deer.

"Anyway, I think it's better if you club it while I hold it down in the net. It doesn't take much, just a few quick blows to the head."

"Henry and June. Otis. Imagine if they met? What would they talk about?" Nola seemed not to be listening to my explanation. Then she shook her head and apologized: "Sorry, go on."

"If we get one in the net," I said, "we have to kill it quickly before its fear spoils the taste of the meat. The young ones sometimes break their legs when I pull them to the ground. They usually bleat, too."

Nola drank the rest of her tea and then set the cup down on the bench. She didn't say anything for a while. She took off Otis's hat and wiped the sweat from her head. She pushed her sunglasses onto the top of her head.

"I think I know what you mean. It's primal," she said in a serious, even voice.

I had never heard the word she used, but from the way she used it, I understood what she meant and took it for consent.

"Yeah, it's like that," I said.

We lay in the grass behind a spread of goldenrod. Ears of corn that I had skewered on stakes were posted on the other side of the goldenrod, close to the edge of the field, where the grasses and weeds merged with the trees of the forest. As we settled into our hiding spot, I heard flies and bees buzzing over us. As the light dimmed in the valley, the chirp of crickets became lower. Our breathing was slow and close. I felt our hips touching, which aroused me. I stretched my neck to kiss Nola, and she opened her mouth as a fish does, moaned silently, and slid her hands under my shirt. I pulled off our pants and moved on top of her, planting my palms on tufts of flattened little bluestem to steady myself. I kept kissing her until her breathing quickened and she began to swallow, trying to contain her groans.

"That's the first time you've climbed on top of me," she whispered when we were done. "You can do that more often, if you want. I like looking up at your face."

We fell asleep with our arms wrapped around each other, our pants half off, down at our calves, ants crawling on our legs.

Later, I awoke to the faint sound of chomping. A wedge of panic rose through me and set me on edge, alert. I had thought the deer wouldn't come, that we could forget about killing one and settle for a lazy meal of vegetables. But now that deer were nearby I wanted to kill one. I crouched, rising just high enough above the goldenrod to see six of them on the fringe of the meadow, with their necks extended, their heads dipping forward under the darkening sky to pull the corn from the sticks.

"They don't notice us," I whispered into Nola's ear and inched my pants up over my hips.

We made our way through the goldenrod, Nola following the silent path I made between the plants. Just before moonlight replaced the dusky sky, a fawn stepped forward, away from its mother, and began nibbling on one of the cobs. We waited until it was taking big bites from the ear of corn. The other deer had moved up meadow to the other stations of bait. Nola slipped her hand through the leather thong of Otis's club. I inched away from her, out of the cover of the goldenrod and through the grass, toward the fawn. The fawn turned its head but seemed not to see me or was unaware of the danger it faced. It returned to pulling the ear of corn off the stake. Nola crept forward and paused and waited for me to take the next step. I weighted the stalks of grass gently, flattening a clump so my toes had a firm purchase to grip as I prepared to sprint.

I stood still, listening to the fawn chew, watching its ears twitch as it shooed away flies. I felt my skin tingling, telling me to rush the deer. I squatted and then burst forward. Within seconds I had accelerated to a low charge, arms outstretched as though I would embrace and wrestle the deer to the ground. The fawn bounded toward the forest, became snagged in a net, and began to jump, further entangling itself. Nola hung back. Otis's club dangled from her wrist. What was she doing? Recording with her hedgehog? Yes. I pulled the net toward the ground, forcing the deer to its knees. Still, Nola didn't approach but continued to record the deer's struggles. The fawn started to bleat, pressing its dark-pink tongue against the net. I could hold it down for only a short time before the old nylon broke. I twisted myself to the side of the fawn to give Nola a clear path to strike.

"Hit it!" I screamed.

She stepped forward and swung Otis's club weakly, landing a blow on the fawn's back. The fawn jerked upwards, splitting the net with its head and opening the skin in the corner of its eye. Blood filled the widening cut.

"The head!" I shouted over the high-pitched bleats of the fawn. I held its front legs and pushed a knee into its rear haunches.

Nola's swings became more focused. She dropped her hedgehog and adopted the posture of someone splitting wood and shrieked each time she connected, in the shoulders, on the neck. When the skull split open, I felt a warm spray of blood on my face. Fluid oozed out of the fawn's nose.

Sweat covered the blond stubble on Nola's sunburned head, her chest pounded as her lungs took in air, and her face was bright pink, nearly bursting. Her teeth showed, not in her customary smile, but in a bare expression that allowed her to pant freely. She looked at me, not speaking, and then stepped back and watched.

I untangled the deer from the net, flipped it onto its back, and drew a line down its abdomen with my knife. I reached my hands up past the heart, severed arteries, and pulled the organs out of the animal's small cavity. I saved the heart for Nola. I approximated Otis's version of a Hidatsa prayer that he said when we killed an animal. I murmured the approximate sounds that were supposed to mean "We accept this and offer thanks in return."

"What did you say?" Nola asked.

"We'll wash it out in the river," I said.

I didn't think she'd understand the prayer, but perhaps I was wrong not to take the time to translate it into English. Perhaps I said it out of habit, of memory, and didn't want to bring Nola fully into the tradition that Otis had created for us.

We dragged the deer through the field, each holding onto a front leg, and I cleaned out the remains of tissue and clotted blood from the opening and scrubbed its head so there were few signs of Nola's strikes. I washed my face.

"You want to carry it over your shoulder? It's your kill," I said.

"It's still wet. I don't think I'd like the feel of that on my body. And I don't want to dirty your grandfather's shirt."

"Then we can carry it by the legs. It's not heavy."

I built a fire in the spot where we had made tea earlier in the day and cooked the heart for her. At first, she wrinkled up her nose at the crisp organ, but after a few bites, she found she liked the taste and ate all of it, afterwards sucking on the end of the olive stick on which I had cooked it.

I fed the fire with driftwood until the bed of coals became thick enough to grill the steaks I had sliced from a haunch. We simmered corn that I had trimmed from the cob. The venison was tender.

Our simple meal wasn't like the ones Otis prepared to celebrate the harvest. Mashed potatoes with onions, garlic, hot peppers; shredded kale dropped in hot water and then mixed with morels; roast corn on the cob and corn cooked with deer fat and sunflower seeds; tortillas smeared with honey: this was the feast we had when the growing season had gone well. Otis sang before we ate, one of his monotonous chants, but in that moment I could tolerate it. At those times I thought our life was perfect, complete.

The coals glowed as though they were breathing. In the faint light I became aware of Nola's fidgeting to find a comfortable position in the dirt.

"I still feel the sensation. One moment it was jerking around, trying to get away, and the next I was smashing its head in. I didn't like the way that felt," she said.

"We don't have to talk about it."

"Why not? Isn't this what you do all the time?"

"I don't usually talk about the killing afterwards."

"But that's what we did, isn't it, kill it? And for what reason?"

"Next time you see a herd of deer in the fields you'll understand."

"I don't know what you're talking about. That there're plenty of deer, that killing just one doesn't matter? I'm glad no one recorded me doing this."

I wasn't sure what I was trying to say. That killing deer was a necessity, part of life? That it was never easy and always filled with a lonely form of fear? I had been much younger than Nola when I had killed my first deer. Even after helping Otis kill them and killing rabbits, grouse, and geese on my own, I had been scared. Nola wasn't ready for this. She had only enthusiasm for killing a deer, no real knowledge of what it entailed. Otis would have been disappointed in my poor judgment and given me a lecture about disrespect, of the deer, of Nola, of myself. Over the years he and I had developed a ritual for carrying out a kill, one that didn't involve talking about it, because we both knew what it took, what it meant, that we had to do it. How could I have expected Nola to know this?

I built up the fire again with the hope that Nola would tell me stories about her life, the way Otis used to when we sat around a fire after a harvest meal, but she didn't. She stared at the flames and watched as the driftwood burned. Maybe she was sorry that she hadn't fixed her boat or was wondering if she'd be punished for taking a break from rowing around the lake. Or for having sex with me. I was afraid to ask and made no effort to entertain her with stories about White Earth River. We let the cool night air and darkness hide us from each other.

Later, when we both started to yawn, she asked, "Do we have to walk up to the cave in the dark? Can't we sleep here?"

The coals would keep us warm enough, and a plastic tarp could serve as a blanket, but the ground would be hard, I told her.

"I don't care," she said.

I let her sleep near the coals while I spooned against her, my back to the darkness. Even though I was holding her, our clothes prevented us from feeling each other's bodies. We didn't make love.

The plastic tarp was stiff and crunched every time we moved during the night. It made me sweat. I felt a great unevenness separating us and causing Nola to drift away. Our lives were too different. Maybe this was as close as we could get. She would leave in the morning, I felt sure, and part of me was glad.

I awoke to a faint whine. It came from downstream and the air carried it up the valley. The sound was too regular and high pitched to be someone singing—the way the stranger had announced his presence. I nudged Nola awake.

"You hear that?" I asked.

She pushed away the plastic tarp and sat up. She rubbed her eyes to clear them of sleep. Dark-blue crescents of skin below her eyes signaled worry and exhaustion. She turned an ear down valley, her mouth drawn in concentration.

"Hmm. No, not really," she said.

"Like a vibration. Far away."

"Could it be insects? Maybe an infestation? Bees?"

"No, they don't sound like that."

"Locusts? Don't they come every so many years?"

"We've never had those."

"I don't know, then."

She yawned and rolled her head to stretch her neck.

"The ground was really hard," she said. "I barely slept."

"It might sound a little like insects," I said, although the faint, even whine was unlike any insect that I'd ever heard.

Nola was standing now. She was scanning the sky down the valley, with her fingers formed like tubes to help her focus her vision. Then she looked at me. Her blue and green eyes were pale, as though the color had been leached out of them. They were not as strong as my dark ones, not able to withstand hours in the midday sun. That's why she needed the sunglasses, I thought, to protect her weak eyes. She rounded her shoulders so her chest seemed to collapse inward. She looked at the ground. I did, too, and saw my crude sandals, my dry and calloused feet. Loneliness passed over me like a cloud moving in front of the sun. It was a familiar if unwanted feeling and always surprised me when it overtook me. But there was something else that accompanied it, now, desire, which mixed things up, not necessarily overpowering loneliness but fighting with it.

"It's a Scout, Pérez."

"A scout?"

"A little plane. Remote controlled. Unpiloted."

She spoke in an even, calm voice.

"They're coming for me," she said. "It must've been launched this morning, after I failed to transmit on schedule. My GPS tracking program would've shown lack of progress. That's why they're looking for me."

I stood up and squinted in the direction from where the sound was coming. Far away against a cloud I saw something that resembled a dragonfly.

"Run. Just get away. Right now," she said.

She seemed to have decided what was going to happen to us. She knew more than I did about the consequences of her action, or misbehavior, if that was what it was in the eyes of the government, and perhaps was trying to protect me. I wanted Otis to speak, to tell me what I should do, but I knew it was too soon. He had waited five years for Malèna to speak to him. "The dead," Otis had explained, "have a lot to learn, just like the newborn. At first all they think about is being dead. Only after they accept that do they have time to contact the living. And the living, they're not ready for the dead. They must learn how to wait, to listen for them."

I wondered if this was what Otis had meant when he said he was practicing, sitting silently on the bench in the garden. I hadn't done this. I'd had to deal with the stranger, with Parshall Bay. And now this. The spaces in my mind shifted, emptied and filled and rearranged themselves. I turned an ear into the wind and listened to the far-off drone of the Scout.

"Nola," I said and grabbed her hand. She didn't answer. Her eyes were large and round. Then I dragged her from the garden, across the road, and down into the basement.

I pushed her down the ladder into darkness, where I lost her until the springs of the metal bed squeaked and revealed her location. How far the sensors and lenses of the Scout could probe I didn't know but imagined we'd be better protected with the wooden panel blocking the entrance.

Thin lines of light fell through the gaps between the cover's slats. I stood guard by the ladder and listened to Nola's sobs, which were muffled by the close, damp air.

"Can they see us through concrete?" I asked.

I felt the cool wall.

"I don't know," she whispered.

"Maybe we should stand away from each other in the center, not close to the walls."

Neither of us moved.

"You nearly dislocated my shoulder," she said. "I think you tore a muscle. My legs are cut up."

I felt my way to the back of the shelter and sat down on the rotting mattress. I wrapped my arms around her and pulled her head against my chest, feeling her fingers dig into my back.

"Can they detect sound?" I asked.

"I'm so stupid," she sobbed.

"If they can detect sound, maybe you shouldn't cry."

The Scout made several passes through the valley. From the increasing intensity of its drone, I guessed that with each pass it was flying lower and lower over the town. I was afraid to move and tensed my body and held Nola so the rusty bed frame wouldn't squeak. Then, the air was still again. I waited a long time before speaking.

"It's gone, now," I said, but at any moment I expected to hear the scraping of the wooden panel as agents kicked it away from the entrance of the basement. We stayed seated on the bed, not moving, and lapsed into another long silence.

After a time, Nola broke the quiet.

"It has my coordinates. It's flying a grid. It won't stop until it pinpoints me. And then Rescue will be alerted. A helicopter will come to take me home. Then I'll be punished. But don't worry. They're only looking for me, not you."

"They won't find us."

"They may already have. Maybe that's why the Scout left. I'd give Rescue half an hour. I'm sure they were on standby."

We spent the rest of the day in the basement, but Rescue never arrived. I don't know whether it was because Otis's concrete construction foiled the Scout or the government decided to give Nola time to contact her advisor. Or maybe the agents, ones high up in government, decided not to look for her. The Scout must have seen her boat tied at the dock and the rumpled tarp laying in the garden, not to mention the crops, perhaps even the carcass of the deer hanging from a cottonwood. The Scout would be back, she assured me, even if her device couldn't transmit in the basement.

Nola began bouncing her knee up and down, as though she were beating time to a song and was about to start singing. The motion made the bed squeak, but she didn't start singing. Perhaps she didn't realize she was doing this. Perhaps the sound of the rusty springs comforted her. Maybe she had forgiven me for pushing her down into the basement. The rhythmic creak of the rusty springs had an odd effect on me, and perhaps Nola, too, because we softened, and I put my arm around her.

"When I was growing up, my grandfather told me that a vision had guided him to the basement, then to the cave, that we were starting a new life, a traditional Hidatsa life. 'The Vision Foretelling the Event and Our Escape to Destiny.' We used to recite the story all the time. First, he to me, then my joining in as I got older. But he had made it all up, the vision. It was just a good story, as it turned out. We happened to be in the basement when the machines came. That's what he confessed right before he died. He never tried to find my parents and warn them, call them back to the basement. They disappeared. It was all an accident. Just an accident."

Nola didn't say anything for a moment, then she said, "We're kind of alike, you and me. You grew up here, safe with your grandfather. I was in the Center, safe with my parents. Meanwhile out there in the continent people were dying and everything was falling apart."

"That's how I got my name."

"How's that?"

"My grandfather called the destruction of the town the Event and named me after it. During-the-Event. It was supposed to be a Hidatsa name. During-the-Event Pérez."

"Something made up and something Spanish."

"A fake name, just like his vision. Just like being Hidatsa. I was the 'first' and the 'last.' That's what he sang in my birth song right before he died. The first Hidatsa to be born in our town, the last to die. Another lie. Who was the last real Hidatsa to die? Not me. Not even my grandfather. He didn't really know who he was, except white, maybe."

My mouth filled with bile, and I spit the sour fluid on the floor.

"History's a burden, Pérez," she said and squeezed my hand, "and we can't outrun it."

I didn't move, but followed the entrance's shaft of light that spread over the floor and the rough walls and revealed the horizontal ridges in the cement, created by the seams of the lumber forms Otis had used, and the matrix of steel beams and galvanized sheeting in the ceiling. How many days had Otis spent in the dim cellar digging alone while the town people passed by and laughed at him? I smelled the minerals in the cement.

At some point early on, I had pleaded with Otis to see the basement. Finally, he had relented and took me there. We had stood in the dark, with the sound of our breathing filling the air. I had expected Otis to say something about his vision, but he only broke our silence by asking, "Have we been here long enough for you?"

Nola took my hand and we lay down. The rusty springs creaked under our weight. The foam mattress launched a gritty cloud into the close air. The dusty shaft of light at the entrance seemed far away.

"My parents were with everyone else, eating deer and drinking, that night," I said.

Nola put her hand over my mouth.

"Hush. It doesn't do any good to remember. Just try to forget."

I let her kiss me but didn't become aroused until she pulled off my pants. We pushed our clothes onto the floor, and I held her tightly as we rocked together on the sour-smelling, rotting foam, only the springs creaking. When we were done, I kept my arms around her. We didn't move but breathed almost as one. We fell asleep with our arms wrapped around each other against the dampness.

Sometime later I woke up and stared at the light coming through the seams in the wood cover. I rose silently and climbed the ladder. I ran to the dock in darkness. I pulled Nola's rowing shell into the boathouse. I didn't want the Scout to see it and think she was still here.

We returned to the cave. Nola couldn't turn off the GPS in her device; it was always on, she said, but keeping the device at the back of the cave and letting the battery drain might prevent the Scout from tracking her to the butte.

The next morning the plane returned and again spent the morning flying a grid over the valley. I worried that the drone might photograph the cave entrance and decided to make the opening look like any other hole in the side of the butte, not someone's home. It hurt me to smash apart the stove and chimney and throw the river rocks and pieces of clay down the butte, to brush the ashes and bits of charcoal over the edge, but I knew that Otis wouldn't have felt remorse, if he'd thought giving up the stove would have allowed him to avoid detection.

As I worked, I wondered if I should leave Nola, run up the valley and hide in a forest or in a collapsing house or the rusted yellow bucket that lay in the grass below the broken wind turbines on top of Windy Butte.

My thoughts troubled me. When Otis became sick, sometimes I wished that he would die, so I wouldn't have to face his demands, the long process of death, the loneliness of living with someone who was no longer whole. Then when he did die, I regretted feeling that way, but I couldn't take back those feelings. The burden of caring for him was lifted, but so was Otis. I didn't want to feel that way again. I wanted Nola to stay.

I was surprised that Nola didn't want to apologize to her advisor for failing to call in, ask for a new pin for her oarlock, and return to thesis, but she didn't. She seemed to have crossed a line and didn't know how to go back. I thought it would be easy for her, a person from the Center, to do so, but she seemed as desperate and fearful as the stranger, as though she, too, had run away. But from what? Perhaps she didn't know how to explain what she had done. Contact with Overlooked was illegal, true. Perhaps making love to one was even more illegal. But how would anyone know? Couldn't she destroy the record of me in her hedgehog and keep silent about our sex? Or was there some way government agents would know we'd had sex? Would a scientist examine her?

I walked to the back of the cave. Nola was lying in my bed and drawing on the back of one of my old arithmetic exercise sheets. She had sketched a picture of an airplane with rockets zooming toward it from a butte. She stopped and looked up at me and narrowed her eyes.

"This was supposed to be *my* project," she said. "I was supposed to have latitude to carry it out as I saw fit. Twenty days. That's all! I could barely breathe when I saw the drone. I bet my parents are behind this. They probably urged my advisor to trigger a search. Such cowards . . .

"Oh, well, it doesn't matter. By now they probably don't consider me in distress or indecisive but actively pursing deceit. A willful disruption of mission, not just poor judgment about the handling of a mishap along the way. Poor judgment can be forgiven if you respond in a way that shows you've recognized your mistake and are taking steps to correct it."

"Tell them you're hurt," I said.

"They wouldn't go for that. You'd have to throw me down the butte for there to be enough evidence. Punishment, that's what I face. I've made myself an outcast, not just an embarrassment to everyone, including myself, but also a failure. I won't be trusted. Won't be able to graduate with my class, take part in the celebrations, or receive a special career assignment. Because I'm female and have good genetic stock, I'll be forced to become a professional breeder. Everyone has to breed, it's a national duty, but some females that's all they do. I'll be like a lab animal, carefully watched as I'm impregnated, gestated, delivered. Singles, twins, triplets. Maybe a batch of quadruplets, if I'm unlucky. I'll have to keep it up for as many years as I can, until my chromosomes start to show signs of age and higher than normal random mutations. Of course, maybe they'll judge my character to be so undesirable that they'll reject me as a breeder. Don't want a re-public full of troublemakers, do we? I might end up on a production preserve."

"I don't see what you did wrong. You only took a day off from rowing."

"You don't know how the Center works. Detours aren't tolerated."

That evening Nola began what she called "the shits." She became pale, and cramps and spasms forced her from the cave to relieve her gut around a corner in a fold of the butte. She blamed her diarrhea on the raw food, foul-tasting well water, unevenly cooked meat, and poor sanitation, things, she said, that her inoculations couldn't pro-tect her from.

I suspected that somehow the currents were responsible for her disease, that it was an extension of her unevenness. The currents had brought all sorts of unhappiness into my life. Otis had protected me from them as long as he could, maybe with the help of his own guardian spirit. I wondered if Otis knew about the singing wolves, that they were the ones who took over after he died. Perhaps out on the lake in the afternoons when I sailed the canoe, before the stranger arrived, I wasn't starting to have a vision but beginning to sense the wolves' presence. And then, in Parshall Bay, the dream had revealed their power to me.

Before it got too dark, that first night of the shits, I descended to the valley and collected bergamot. At least this would treat the symptoms of Nola's illness, even if it were useless against what the currents had set in motion.

During this time I worried about being able to complete the harvest alone. The harvest was usually a period of hard work and long days in which Otis and I became closer. I never imagined I would harvest the first crop of corn after he died under these conditions: risking the threat of detection by a Scout while someone I barely knew recovered from illness in the cave.

My attention toward Nola diminished, perhaps because we weren't sexing and I suspected she'd leave me. She seemed to be slipping away, retreating into herself, whereas I began to think about what we would do once the harvest was complete.

We passed the daylight hours by sleeping, reading children's stories, and looking at the black book of photographs of Otis and Malèna and the blue booklet of the Sierra Madre Occidental farmers. Only once did I hear a Scout fly low through the valley. Its sound silenced us, froze us in place, as though our movement could be detected, our voices heard, our body heat sensed, even though we were at the back of the cave. Was it surveying the garden, tracking my progress with the harvest, to determine whether we were still in White Earth River? And then it left.

At night I'd descend from the cave to finish the harvest. I worked naked, both to stay cool and to blend in with the landscape. I cut down sunflower and bean plants and draped them along with the braids of corn over the roof of the monorail car, where they could bake undetected, drying out more quickly than they would in the field. I carved up the fawn in long strips and laid the meat over the red seats, keeping the door closed so flies wouldn't contaminate it.

My eyes adjusted to a world of dim star- and moonlight, and I navigated this terrain by touch, memory, and error. Food was plentiful, but I couldn't enjoy it. I ate almost as though I were in the middle of the cool season.

While alone in the dark fields of the garden, I started to think that the only option was to leave White Earth River and hide out in a new valley, one unknown to the Scout and where no one would look for us. Then we would head south. The Badlands along the Little Missouri River had been a feature of Otis's stories about the history of the Hidatsa. We would be safe there. When I told Nola about the Badlands, she asked, "Do you think we have enough food to get there?" "We can carry quite a bit in the canoe, especially if it's dried," I answered.

This was the only exchange we had on the subject.

Nola always waited for me to return to the cave before going to sleep. To help her relax, I drummed softly against a cottonwood post or massaged the shoulder that I had hurt when I dragged her from the garden and down into the basement.

One night in the middle of my drumming, I said, "I don't like this, living only at night."

"Once my malaise passes and I regain my strength. A few more days," she said.

Then she said, "You know your book, the one about the farmers in the Sierra Madre?"

"Yeah."

"Well, those people aren't related to your father. Your father has Indian blood, several types of it, and Spanish blood, too, but he's not Tarahumara, like the farmers in the book. A lot of people from Mexico and South America have mixed blood. Very few are pure, Pérez."

"You don't know that."

"Of course I know that. The analysis of your blood proved it."

"You said it'd take awhile."

"The results came in while you were collecting honey. I didn't tell you because I didn't want you to feel bad, since it seemed important to you to believe that your father was from the Sierra Madre Occidental. But I'm telling you now because I don't know what will happen. I want to tell you something else, too."

"Okay."

"Your mother was one hundred percent Italian. One hundred percent. Do you know how rare it is to be one hundred percent?"

Why had Nola waited until this moment to tell me? Perhaps she'd never intended to reveal what she'd found about my parents but then changed her mind. Maybe she understood that the cave was where stories were created and shattered and wanted somehow to be part of this tradition. Or maybe she was trying to warn me that the government knew all about me now, and that the Scout wasn't *just* looking for her.

I drummed loudly for a few minutes to force an end to our conversation. Then I took off my shorts and shirt and climbed into Otis's bed beside her. She slipped off her rowing shorts and the heavy navy sweater of Otis's that she had been wearing. Her body felt cool to me, and I hugged her and drew the rabbit-skin blanket over us and held her until she was warm.

The red canoe held the dried corn, not the entire harvest, of course, as well as the dried venison, sunflower seeds, and beans; as many fresh vegetables as I thought we could eat before they became limp and inedible; and a few tools and supplies. With our heavy load secured between the bow and stern, our progress down the river, across the bay, and along the shore of Lake Sakakawea was slow. I left the sail behind, so we'd have more room in the canoe for food; once we reached the Little Missouri, we wouldn't have been able to use the sail, anyway.

It took two nights to reach the Van Hook Arm, where we camped in a grove of elms on the southern shore. The next night we continued east, to what Nola was fairly sure was the mouth of the Little Missouri River, the route to the Badlands, which Otis had told me was so rugged and remote—impenetrable was the word he had used—that no one could track people who hid there.

We stopped paddling well before sunrise. Already I felt lost in the maze of coves that obscured the transition from Lake Sakakawea to the main channel of the Little Missouri River. I guided us into a narrow inlet and searched for a landing where we wouldn't leave footprints or a skid mark from the canoe. I helped Nola struggle up an embankment to tall cottonwoods, away from the grasses so we wouldn't have to worry as much about snakes. It was a miserable way to spend the day, swatting insects and sitting still in the heat, trying to sleep under the deerskin. I prayed to the singing wolves to not let satellites spot the tracks we had made through the grass.

"You think they're still searching for you?" I asked.

"I don't know," she said. "By now they probably think I'm dead. We haven't heard or seen anything since the last Scout. That could've been sent to confirm their suspicions of no activity."

"We haven't given them anything to find. And soon we'll be in a place where they aren't looking."

Patches of low clouds started to gather in the afternoon, leaving just enough of an opening in their coverage to allow light from a less than full moon to help us navigate. Even though I was steering the canoe, I was glad that Nola sat in the bow, as if she were the one guiding us across the water in the dark. Her paddle barely made a sound as she dipped it into the water and drew it along the hull of the canoe.

I heard Nola set the blade of her paddle across the gunwales to rest. She turned toward me. The moonlight caught her face.

"Pérez?" she said. "It feels like we're really far away. I mean, farther away than we've been so far."

"We're just starting up the Little Missouri. Land is all around us. It's the darkness that makes you feel that way," I said.

"No, that's not what I mean. I know where we are. I remember the maps. But this feels different. Maybe it's knowing that the Scouts aren't interested in me anymore, that they've let me go, said goodbye."

"We're just floating. Paddling and floating. Once we get to the Badlands and it's daylight, you'll feel different. We'll be somewhere."

"Maybe."

After several hours of slow paddling, we reached a section of the river where I couldn't tell whether the main channel ran east or west. Rather than risk making a mistake, I pulled ashore and hid the canoe under willows. We walked up a valley to a terrace and spread a deerskin under some scrubby oaks. This was a drier and cooler site than our other camps had been, and we were able to sleep until morning, when the rain started. Lying beneath the deerskin reminded me of becoming soaked and cold and dreaming of the singing wolves. This time I didn't shiver but stayed entwined with Nola, our body heat keeping us warm under the damp hide. When we were together like this, in each other's arms, I could forget what had happened and pretend that we had never been discovered, that Nola was not pre-occupied with her fears. When night fell, we reentered the river and drifted in darkness while I tried to gauge our movement against the black shore.

"My hedgehog could tell us which direction to go," she said.

"You don't need a hedgehog to detect current," I said.

"Don't worry, it's packed away. It hasn't charged," she said.

In that moment I believed her. I felt the water pushing against my paddle, suggesting a westward turn of the river. The channel narrowed, the inlets became fewer and shallower, and the bends began to loop back and forth in a predictable pattern. The current finally revealed its strength. Nola turned to me and said, "I don't feel like we're getting anywhere." I dug my paddle into the water and encouraged her to do the same.

In the soft pre-morning light I could tell that the landscape would conceal us well and landed the canoe on a wide gravel beach. All around us the buttes were severe, layered, and widespread, more jagged and steep than the two framing the White Earth River. Canyons, ridges, and outcrops seemed to stretch to the horizon. If a Rescue helicopter could manage to land on one of these features, the pilot would become lost as soon as he stepped from the cockpit.

I unloaded the canoe and carried our provisions into the thick, cottonwood-covered bottomland that was only a short run from the spine of a butte. This would be our escape route, if we needed one, I thought. Out of habit, I tied the canoe to a sapling with a section of the faded and frayed yellow rope, even though the boat was far enough from the river that only a flood would wash it downstream.

I chanced making a small fire, hoping its smoke would go unnoticed by any satellites or Scouts still passing overhead. I sliced fresh corn from a cob to make a mush and tossed in tomatoes and carrots for a change.

"A long time ago Indians spent the winters down along the river bottoms in the cottonwoods to stay out of the wind and to hunt buffalo," I said as I prepared our meal. "They'd call them to their camps and then kill them. That's what Otis said, anyway."

"Go ahead and try. I'm sure we're isolated enough that your yelling wouldn't draw any attention," Nola said. She was resting against a tree trunk, her legs stretched out.

"There probably aren't any buffalo left anyway. Elk, maybe. We could try to call them, if we knew what sound they liked."

"I don't think I'm ready to tangle with an elk, considering a little deer gave me so much trouble. Maybe I should just drink the rest of the powder. After all, I'm probably not going to finish thesis."

"To celebrate daylight, maybe," I said, hoping to humor her, so she'd feel happy about our new life together. "But I can always try to catch a walleye later, too."

"I should probably save the powder for an emergency."

We shared the pot of mush, blowing on steaming spoonfuls before placing them in our mouths and chewing the soft, warm vegetables.

"I'm famished," Nola said.

"It doesn't bother your stomach?"

"No, food seems to help. Maybe I get nauseous because I'm empty."

"But you're feeling better?"

"It comes and goes. I've never had anything like this."

"I was worried about you."

"I wasn't sure. At first you weren't saying much."

"You were so pale, you still are, and we couldn't make love."

"I thought you were mad at me."

She sounded sad, and I felt guilty for thinking about running away and leaving her behind. I took leaves of chard, spooned mush along their central veins, and rolled them up.

"I knew I had to be strong for both of us," I said. "I'm sorry the harvest didn't last longer. It's usually a happy time."

"The first day was good," she said. "Even killing the deer, I guess. I'm probably the first person in the Center to have that experience."

"Probably." I handed her a leaf of chard. "You need fresh greens."

She seemed older, her voice quieter, flatter; her hair had taken on a dirty color and was no longer golden fuzz.

"I need everything. I can't believe we're here."

"I can. I knew if I concentrated, we'd make it. Plus, I asked the singing wolves to look after us."

"I was wondering about that."

I stretched out across from Nola on the soft duff of cottonwood leaves and old grasses. I had grown so accustomed to living in darkness that it seemed as though we had been dropped through a cloud into this Badlands valley, with no memory of how we had arrived and no clue about how to leave. It was a reassuring sensation, I decided, like being in the cave, cut off from the world.

"You know, when we were paddling, I started to think," I said, "that there're two types of people, those who make plans, and those who see patterns. But very few do both."

Nola laughed, the first time since we had gone into hiding.

"And this is based on, what, knowing three people?" she asked.

"Yeah, but I know about more than three people," I said.

"What five, six? Maybe eight?" She laughed again. I liked hearing the ring in her voice.

"No, listen. My grandfather thought he saw patterns, but he didn't. He was just making them up, and so he was stuck with his plans. The stranger was the same. He had only plans, which weren't much good against forces he couldn't control."

"His drowning, you mean?"

"Yeah, the currents." I took a bite of the chard roll.

"And you're different?"

"Me and you. We can see patterns. And make plans. That's why we're going to survive. Maybe that's what my grandfather meant when he sang that I was the last and the first. The last one to survive because I was the first one to see things this way."

Nola finished chewing her chard and mush and then spoke: "That's quite a philosophy. You could be a professor." She sat up straight and crossed her legs. "I think I'd like a little deer meat. That'd be okay, don't you think?"

"It's fairly tough."

"I'll just suck on it, soften it up. I feel like something tough and stringy. I need to get my muscles back."

I untied the deerskin in which I had wrapped the meat and took out a handful of strips and dropped them into the pot. I began to work on a piece with my back teeth. After a while, Nola paused in chewing and pointed her strip of meat at me.

"I didn't know your grandfather," she said, "and don't know if he really would've cared much about patterns. He certainly could make plans. All successful people do. His photographs showed that he was accomplished. And that he enjoyed life. I think he wanted you, too, to enjoy life."

I sucked on the dried venison and gnawed off a small piece. I savored its sharp taste.

"His photographs helped him remember his old life," I said.

188

"I'm sure they did. But when he died, he seemed to be giving up not only the life you shared but also some of the delusions he had created about it, while still holding onto a few that would make dying easier. 'First' and 'last,' I think he was probably speaking literally. You were the first and last person to be raised the way you were, in your grandfather's experience, at least. His acknowledgment of that was his way of saying, 'Okay, now it's time to go out and create your own life because this one is over.'"

I felt angry that Nola was speaking about Otis as though she knew what he had been thinking. Her tone of voice didn't suggest that she was being disrespectful of him, only that she knew something that I didn't, that perhaps even Otis didn't know. It was as if she had made a sudden movement that I hadn't anticipated and couldn't counter, and for a few minutes I didn't know how to react. Then I said:

"It's not over. Our life, Otis's and mine. I'm just moving it to a safer place. I could start a garden here, if I wanted. I could build a house here, too. In fact, I think I like this valley better than the White Earth River valley. Or we could travel south and find my father's family."

"Okay, okay. Yeah, you could do any one of those things. But, really, why?"

At first I nearly blurted out, "I like looking at these buttes." She had questioned such a fundamental aspect of my nature. Then I wanted to say, "Because it's who I am," but that seemed more stupid and inadequate than an observation about buttes. So I said:

"It's what I know."

"Yeah, okay, sure, that's true. It's been your life up to now. But I think you were destined for greater things."

Nola was sitting up, now, no longer lying on her side, with her hand propping up her head. She had more color in her face. Her voice was lively again, the way it was when we met on the water, before we went into hiding. Did this make me happy? No, Nola sounded as though she were trying to imitate Otis. Our conversation was making the air sharp, threatening the pleasant safety of the cottonwood grove. I sat up, too, and said: "What do you mean?"

"You know the way I've been feeling nauseous? Well, I've been thinking. I might be pregnant."

"What?" I shouted. "It's not possible, is it?"

"I don't know. My breasts have been a little sore, too."

"I haven't touched them in over a week."

"I'm sure it's not from you. You're gentle, suckling like a little lamb."

Nola laughed—at me it felt like. I was furious.

"I am not a little lamb!" I shouted.

After all my work, hiding us in the cave, caring for Nola, harvesting the crops at night, navigating to this isolated valley in the Badlands, she begins to talk happily about impossibilities—pregnancy.

"Oh, Pérez, you're so serious. I'm sorry. It makes me laugh."

She covered her mouth to conceal her chuckling.

"But imagine, Pérez, if I *am* pregnant, it would be a special child, yours and mine, a predominantly European genotype with exceptional coloring. I think everyone would be very satisfied, especially my father. My mother, too. She might be less sad as a grandmother. It would be a free child, a bonus, one that didn't cost the government anything. No search for eggs and sperm, no lab expenses, no surrogate. Of course, I'd want to have it in the Center. I'd want it to have a perfect navel."

"Malèna died in a hospital in the Center."

"I could call my father and ask him to negotiate for us."

"I thought you said it was too late."

"A baby would redeem me, reunite me with my father and mother. An unexpected end to thesis, but a positive outcome nonetheless."

"I don't think so."

"You have unique DNA, Pérez, your history and experience, too. It's a sign of fitness and desirability. They'd match you with other women."

"I don't want to make love to other women."

"Just ejaculate into a cup. That's all guys do. You have thousands, millions of sperm in one sample. Enough for an army of Pérez's!"

"I'm not doing it in a cup, either."

What happened next embarrasses me. It's hard for me to admit to myself that Nola's and my conversation about pregnancy and ejaculating into a cup aroused me. I know it's pathetic that such stupid talk about things I had no interest in could make me desire her. My lack of self-control disgusts me, but there I was, placing my half-eaten strip of deer meat in the pot and moving close to Nola. I put a hand against her sunburned cheek and kissed her rough lips.

"Wait," I said.

I unrolled the patchwork of hides, the one in which I had wrapped Otis to tow him to the grave. I didn't tell Nola about the history of the deerskin, and risk breaking the spell of arousal. I spread it on the ground. She scooted onto the skin and lay down on her back. She worked her hand between the buttons of my shirt and began to stroke my chest. I took in the scent of her unwashed body and the smell of venison on her breath.

I shed my clothes and helped her remove hers. Our lovemaking wasn't frantic, as it had been the first time or even subsequent times in the fields and in the basement, but it was pleasurable. The memory of it still gives me joy. How could I be so mad one moment about her suggestion that I become a breeder and the next moment want to make love to her?

When Nola and I had finished, I rolled onto my back and held her against me, her head resting on my chest. I could feel the stubble on her head, longer and softer, now. Her hair was starting to grow back.

"You did it this time, Pérez," she said, "I'm sure."

I squeezed her against me and let my thoughts drift. We should stay here. I could transfer all we needed from White Earth River, then I'd split apart the canoe with the ax. Pregnant, Nola wouldn't be able to walk overland to the Center; she wouldn't even know the way. I looked up at the undersides of the cottonwood leaves and watched them tremble. I would know how to raise a child. Except for my earliest years, I remembered everything.

"Roll up the blanket. Wedge it under me." Nola interrupted my thoughts.

"What?"

I began to laugh as Nola raised her pelvis up into the air.

"I want your sperm to settle deep down inside of me. Get it past my cervix, up into my fallopian tubes. Store it, give me the best chance."

I shoved the blanket under her buttocks.

"I might have some eggs loose, first hatch scouting for sperm."

I laughed again at the position Nola had assumed.

"Okay, while you're waiting for my sperm to swim upstream, I'll take a walk and try to find us a spring. We'll need clean water so you don't get sick again."

"Find something that tastes better than your dirty old well, Pérez."

I left her on the deerskin and followed the shore of the river around a bend until it ended at a cut bank where the river had churned into the earth. I climbed up through loose dirt to what seemed like an overgrown path. It was wider than a game trail. I could tell that it had been there, well above the bends of the river and the seasonally flooded bottomland, for a long time. People, horses, or perhaps cattle had worn the trail into the ground through their comings and goings, perhaps to pasture, perhaps to the river for water. It was narrower than it had once been, but the well-trodden track was still easy to follow. I saw the footprints of deer, mice, rabbits, raccoons, and, every so often, coyotes. All sorts of animals used it.

The trail passed along the edges of the bottomland, while rugged buttes rose above me. After hiding in the cave and working at night, I craved the sunlight. The proportions of the valley were pleasing, and I walked fast. As I moved upstream, the buttes became more spread out and patches of shrubs and bands of trees stretched over the hills. From the top of a rise, I could see the flat prairie lying before me to the south, the path a line to the horizon. This was the route we would take to the Sierra Madre Occidental—when the baby was old enough to travel.

I liked what I saw: a valley with a history of human use, which seemed to prove that we would be able to stay here and plant a garden. I liked the broadness of the valley, too, how it expanded from the canyons of the Badlands. This gave me hope. Although I hadn't found a spring, I felt confident that one was uphill. I turned and jogged downstream toward camp to tell Nola what I had found.

She wasn't lying on the deerskin. At first I thought that the food had made her sick and she had wandered into the cottonwood stand to vomit. I called her name several times, but she didn't answer. I searched for her in larger and larger circles, eventually ending up at the gravel beach.

The yellow rope snaked from the sapling through grass to the edge of the river, where its frayed end floated in the water. A line through the sand left by the keel showed where Nola had pushed the canoe into the river. Perhaps I had been away too long and she had gotten scared and gone to look for me. Once in the current, she wouldn't have had the strength to paddle upstream and would have been taken downstream toward the bay. I had to catch her before she drifted into one of the wide arms of the river, out of sight and shouting distance.

I picked up a path above the river, down from our camp, and began running north, toward Lake Sakakawea. As I ran, I thought of the singing wolves and hoped they were guarding Nola, even if she didn't believe in them. I recited the simple prayer that Otis and I had said when we hunted: "We accept this and give thanks in return." And then began rearranging the words: "We take this and give thanks for it." "We give thanks for living." "We offer ourselves in return."

I thought: If she were not in any of the inlets or the bay, I would start swimming. Once she heard my shouts, she would paddle toward me. Then I would never let her out of my sight.

The path ended on the bank of an inlet. Nola wasn't on the water. She didn't answer my shouts. I didn't start swimming. The inlet was vast, larger than I had imagined it to be when we had paddled its length in the dark. The canoe was nowhere along the shore. I had lost her. She was gone.

PART VI: COACHELLA VALLEY (ALICE AND GEORGE)

Something in me broke that moment as I stared out across the empty surface of the water. The feelings that welled up in my body told me that Nola hadn't gone to look for me upstream and hadn't been swept away; she'd stolen the canoe and paddled downstream to the lake, where she could float in the open water and call to be rescued. Her device still worked—that was never in question—she had only chosen not to charge it in the sun. Perhaps she had charged it that morning when we woke up in daylight in the Badlands. Perhaps she had been charging it all along while I was sleeping or working in the valley. Or maybe the laser cylinder that she called "protection" had enough power to signal the military. Agents could have been following us at night in a boat and had rescued her as soon as I walked upstream. Or what if she had tried to paddle away, capsized, and drowned, as the stranger had, and the currents had claimed her?

Whatever happened didn't really matter. She was gone and, if pregnant, had taken part of me along with her. I began to feel as though she had tricked me.

I could have walked around the lake until I came to White Earth Bay. It would have taken days, maybe weeks, but I could have done it. I chose not to. The thought of returning saddened me. Dread of the place filled me. Too much misfortune had occurred there. It wasn't a place to make a home, despite the garden and cave. Nola had caused the valley to be discovered, and now it was ruined. I'd never again be safe there. I never wanted to go back. I would set out alone to find my father's homeland.

If Mexico was now part of the continental government, as Nola said it was, perhaps my father had been allowed to return. Maybe he wasn't from the Sierra Madre Occidental, but the Tarahumara might know where I could look for him. And if they didn't, I could ask them to take me in. I didn't want to work a garden alone until I was an old man and had to lower myself into a hole and wait to die. I headed south. I had nothing to lose.

At first I followed the Little Missouri River upstream, with as much food as I could carry in the deerskin lashed to my back with the yellow rope. Sometimes I walked through fields of dry grass along the shore. Other times I had to climb around a bluff and track the river from a distance until the river bank reemerged with the path. The river was muddy, but I drank it anyway. There were plenty of walleye to catch. Eventually, I came to a bridge where a road ran straight south. The river flowed east. I gambled that I'd be able to find water and gather edible plants, that my supply of dried corn and venison would last until I got somewhere, and that I wouldn't be killed if I encountered people. From time to time along the side of this road were rusted signs with the number 85 in faded black. There were other signs, too, names of empty towns of which I'd never heard.

I found a bicycle at an abandoned farm whose land was eroded and dried out. The house didn't smell bad, and the beds were made up. I stayed there while I taught myself to ride the bike. Cycling was much faster than walking, and I could see why the stranger had preferred traveling in this way. I stuck to road 85 and headed south through dry grasslands, which looked as though they were recovering from fire. I risked pedaling throughout the day, despite the afternoon heat and my worry of encountering government agents. I never saw anyone. At least the breeze the bicycle generated cooled me some.

Then, I saw a herd of animals. At first I didn't know what they were. I figured they were wild, but then I saw a truck with a trailer and several men on horses. They wore tan pants and shirts and hats. Their faces were different colors: brown, white, and black. I wasn't afraid because they seemed to be farmers. One of them, a man with a white face, rode to the highway and looked me up and down. He asked what tribe I was from. "Tarahumara," I said. And why not? Maybe some of my father's Indian blood was Tarahumara. "Right on, brother, we're Oglala Sioux."

This man's name was Willy. His tribe grazed a large herd of goats between their reservation and the Oglala and Thunder Basin grasslands. Because these areas had once been parks, the forage was still good. The government hadn't bothered to close down the reservation, Willy told me.

"It wasn't a question of sovereignty. Government has never had a problem with exterminating Indians, whether through outright slaughter or a proxy war conducted by the breweries and distilleries. Turned out we were pretty damn good goat herders. Guess we adapted some of the old ways. And then there was the amnesty."

This was the first I had heard of the amnesty. Nola hadn't told me about it, perhaps because she wanted to control my choices and persuade me to come to the Center with her. Or maybe she didn't even know about it, because it wouldn't have concerned her.

"Supposedly, government needs everybody, now," Willy said. "No reprisals if you present yourself. Food, shelter, job, reproduction. That's what they say." What he said did seem to agree with what Nola had told me: there was now a population shortage after the government killed too many people.

"New people have been showing up at the reservation. Some claim a percentage of Sioux in their lineage, but honestly, we accept anyone who wants to work. Can't really say what's happening farther south where you're going. The southwest was headed for decimation from the beginning. The heat—you only have so many layers of clothes you can take off."

The Oglala had crops, too, and hunted on the open prairie and fished in a lake they kept stocked with catfish. They fueled their old trucks with oil pressed from corn. They delivered goats to a market south of them, in Fort Collins, in former Colorado.

They hadn't heard of my father and didn't know about the Tarahumara but were interested in the blue booklet. They asked me to join their tribe. When I declined, they convinced me to stay with them until the peak of the warm season had passed. They taught me how to watch the goats and shoot a rifle, though the dogs kept the coyotes away at night and I never had to kill one.

I studied old maps of the states that used to make up the continent. In the workshop a woman helped me build a cart to haul food and water and adjusted the gear ratio on my bike so it would be more suitable for climbing hills. She gave me a spare pump to keep the tires full so the wheels would roll faster. After a couple of months of tending goats, I loaded the bike and cart in the back of a truck and rode with Willy to Fort Collins to deliver a trailer full of goats to the slaughterhouse.

Willy told me to stick to the mountains as much as possible. Their valleys would be cooler than open plains, despite the die-offs of trees from pests and forest fires, and there'd be a greater chance of predictable and unpolluted water, he said. He showed me a network of roads down the Rockies and through a patchwork of forests. This route would be less populated, he assured me, with fewer government patrols.

"It's hard to say what you'll encounter. I don't know about the southwest, or the tribes there. But I guess if you show up, they'll probably take you in, if anyone's left. Try to get to the Utes in southern Colorado. They'll know what lies ahead."

Willy let me keep the maps, and I pedaled south. The route had many long climbs up to passes followed by terrorizing descents for which the bike's brakes barely slowed me. The cart clattered and bounced and made cornering dangerous. I had the benefit of the fat reserve I had built up while with the Oglala, and plenty of dried goat, corn meal, and sunflower seeds, which after a time I dreaded eating. Water was mostly not a problem, although some of it had to be bad—diarrhea hit me a few times and left me weak and sad.

I arrived at the lands of the Ute at night. The bright red sign of the casino alerted me to their home. I spent several nights there. Not in the casino itself but outside a house of one of the workers, a card dealer. He offered me a job, which I refused. The casino had remained a destination because of the energy workers. First it had been the natural gas miners, and now it was the solar people. I had seen acres of the panels wherever overhead wires crossed the highway, which they did every so often.

The Ute were not of much help. They of course were kind hosts and gave me big jugs of water and plenty of canned food, which made my cart heavy and difficult to pull, but they offered little advice about the route to Mexico. They said there was a lot of Indian land but not that many Indians; after the amnesty, the survivors had migrated to energy, mining, and water preserves, where there were jobs, food, and water. They laughed at my goal, to reach the Tarahumara, and told me that I'd probably die instead. Their word of caution: "Avoid what used to be Arizona as much as possible. It's really hot, even in winter." (Winter was their word for the cool season.) "And stock up on water every chance you get, even if it's brown."

Thomas, the casino worker with whom I stayed, said: "If you're going to Mexico, go to Baja. It's paradise. Beautiful beaches. Tasty fish. Rest there until you're ready to head inland."

"There's a road?" I asked.

"Sure, why not?" he said. "There're always roads, aren't there?"

I pedaled through the nights. When the moon waxed, I traveled far. When it waned, I covered fewer kilometers. In the mountains, where the nights were cool, pedaling kept me warm. During the day I rested under a nylon tarp that was slowly deteriorating from the sun. I held onto the hot metal tubes of the bicycle as I lay on the warm ground. This made me want to hold Nola. Sometimes I thought how I had touched three humans in my life, Nola, the stranger, and Otis. All in different ways.

Some nights I saw other Overlooked. If they were on foot, they scurried off into bushes or hid behind a tree or ran toward the horizon until I passed. A few were on bicycles. We stopped and exchanged greetings, sometimes food or water. One man asked me if I had heard about the amnesty. He wanted to turn himself in because he was tired of the heat and living in a dry world. He wanted air conditioning and cold water. But like me he was suspicious, and at the end of our conversation we both got on our bikes and headed in opposite directions.

Other nights I heard the hum and vibration of trucks passing on the road above my camp. If there was adequate moonlight, I could see images painted on the sides of the trucks: vegetables, fruits, and animals. These caravans of food were accompanied by military patrols. I don't know whom they thought was going to attack the trucks, especially in the empty lands that I pedaled through, but their guns were ready. Could they have seen me, lying on the ground under my tarp? Or would they have passed before my disruption in the landscape registered in their minds?

I pedaled west, taking a route above the Colorado River as I tried to avoid the heat and dryness of Arizona. Whenever I saw a patch of green in the distance, I'd pedal toward it, if there were a road. Green represented irrigation or a spring, even an unattended one. I became sick of the blue sky. It never changed unless there was a dust storm, and then I couldn't breathe. Sometimes I'd look to the horizon and be thankful for a tan sky, even if it meant trouble was on its way.

The only persons I saw while crossing through Navajo lands were two men in a car. They were going home after a month in Las Vegas on a project to convert hotels to dormitories for energy workers. Las Vegas was the center of energy production in the southwest, nuclear but a lot of solar, too, though that tended to be more dispersed, they said. They filled one of my jugs of water.

The Kaibab Indians, just south of the old Utah border, were not hopeful about my plans to follow the Colorado down through the desert to former Mexico. They thought everyone I had met along the way, starting with the Sioux, had made a mistake in advising me. The Sioux shouldn't have let me continue south, they said. The blue booklet about the Tarahumara was old. They doubted this group of people still existed. Lack of water and heat, as simple as that. Even if they were exceptional, they couldn't conquer these elements, which were more powerful than earth, wind, and fire.

I rested with them and studied maps, yet the maps yielded no secrets. They advised me how to skirt Las Vegas and find route 95, which ran south to where I could cross into former Mexico and then on to Sonora and into Chihuahua. The border, they assured me, would present no problems if I survived to cross it. The language would be different once I arrived, although probably the people who were still living also spoke English, but perhaps with a different accent. Along the way, seek out the Hualapi and Colorados, if any are left; they would help you, they said.

For the most part I followed their advice. But I ran out of water and detoured west to Nipton—an abandoned community with a still-working well. A dirt road with a washboard surface led south through the Mojave. I thought it would take me to Mexico. Perhaps I was delirious from dehydration by then. The road ended at a track running southwest–northeast. I set off toward the southwest. Deserted buildings dotted the way. Stores had been emptied of supplies. Water faucets offered only the creaking of their handles but no water. This part of the trip was necessary, perhaps the last efforts of the singing wolves to prepare me to leave the realm of their protection before I entered the providence of George and Alice. If I hadn't taken this route, I would never have met George and Alice and surely would have died.

I nearly did die. As I was coasting down the San Gorgonio pass that morning, from the high desert to the valley floor, a blast of wind made me lose control. The bike and cart overturned, and I hit the ground. I don't know how long I was unconscious. When I awoke, the long blades of wind turbines were slicing thick, dusty air. Their violent humming sounded like a storm. My head throbbed. I was afraid to move. This is where I'll die, I thought, far from home, where Otis's spirit can't find me.

After a while, I heard the crunch of gravel, a metal door opening, footsteps on the pavement. A man bent over me. He wore a cowboy hat like the one Otis used to wear, although Otis's was more creased and beat up, with frayed holes in the crown. The man had white hair and skin that was dark red from the sun. This, as it turned out, was George. Once he determined that I could move all my limbs, he helped me to his truck and drove me to the wind farm in the Coachella Valley.

I had to stay in bed for a few days. My head had split open on the pavement, but the blood loss and gash—a long line of stitches—weren't as worrisome as the headache, which persisted for days and left me confused. A bruised hip and backache made me limp for several weeks, during which time I mostly slept and ate the light meals that Alice delivered to my house.

Once all my pain was gone and I had started spending the day talking to Alice in the kitchen, George called me into his office.

"Here's the situation, Perry," he said, using the nickname he had given me. "I need a gardener. We're trying to get some vegetables started, add some variety to our meals. Sunlight isn't a problem, obviously, and neither is water, really. We're generating enough power to drain the rest of the aquifer. It's just that no one so far seems to have a green thumb, except Alice, but she doesn't have time to cook and garden."

I looked at my thumbs, which were brown like the rest of my skin.

"It's an expression," George said, "you know, about one's ability to grow plants?"

"I can grow plants," I admitted.

"Okay, then what do you say? If you don't want to be the gardener, I can try to find a place for you on a service team. We're full up right now at the wind farm. I might have to send you up to Nuevo Sacramento for a time. They always need workers, especially ones adapted to the heat."

"A production preserve."

"Central Valley ag. Old corporate farms, not bad."

"I'm not living on a production preserve."

"Or I could send you down to Angeles del Este. They always need factory workers. We send them energy."

"I'm not working in a factory."

"Then it's settled. You're my gardener. I'll have to enter you into the system, of course. And someone from Demographics will have to interview you, take some DNA. You'll still have to fulfill your national reproductive service obligation."

"I think I already did that."

"When?"

"A while ago, in my valley."

"You don't look old enough."

"Seventeen or eighteen, Nola said."

"Okay. You fooled me. Pregnancy confirmed?"

"I don't know. We weren't together for very long."

"Well, in any case, whatever you did probably wasn't official. I'll note it nonetheless. Maybe buy you some time to find someone you like, so you can avoid a government selection. Nola, huh? Nola what?"

"Just Nola. She was from the Center."

"Oh, a high-class girl. You've had some luck, then."

"She took my blood, too."

"Then maybe the government already knows about you. I can check."

A gardener. Work that I knew, though I wasn't thinking about work just yet. My mind was still somewhere between White Earth River and the wind farm, moments of my life replaying themselves like one of Nola's short videos on her device. The hope of reaching Mexico had faded when I crashed, but had it died? Could I fix my broken bike and pedal through a desert until I found people? George didn't seem to be giving me many choices. Perhaps if I left he'd call an agent.

A few nights later George asked me to take a walk with him. He wanted to discuss expanding the garden, he said. As we moved away from the light of the kitchen, he filled a tiny pipe from a leather pouch. He lit the pipe with a match and drew on the stem. He held the smoke in his lungs and then exhaled in a long, steady breath. The wind chimes that Alice had hung in the garden, perhaps to scare off crows, rang in the faint breeze. We reached the end of the garden, where its fence met the open desert. George still hadn't spoken and neither had I. He leaned against a fence post and looked out into the desert. Shrubs and jackrabbits were out there, I knew. I gazed up at the stars. Finally, he spoke: "Well, Perry, you're in the database."

"Nola," I said.

"Yep. Ordered up your whole story."

"She told me right before she left me. A Scout had been looking for her."

"Not surprising. Most Overlooked would kill an elite, if they had the chance. Government probably thought she was endangered."

"I wasn't a threat."

"Course you weren't, Perry."

"But that's how people saw me."

"Thought you were outside of history, huh?"

Nola's story about outrunning history played in my mind, but I didn't tell George.

"I understand from Alice that you were looking for your father," George said. "Or his people down in old Mexico."

I didn't say anything.

"What's it been? Twenty years?"

"Maybe eighteen. I was a baby when they disappeared."

"It was a bad time, twenty years ago. Attempts to overthrow the government. Government fought back mercilessly. A lot of people were killed. Too many. That's why we have the amnesty. 'Controlled regrowth,' is what they call it.

"There's no record of them, your folks, only your DNA. Anything could have happened to them. Shot the night they disappeared. Split up and shipped off to work, if they had desirable skills. Died on the job. It's pointless to look. You'll never find out what happened."

We stood, silent on the edge of the garden. The air had become a couple degrees cooler. I gripped two squares in the wire fence. My eyes had adjusted to the darkness, and I could make out the shape of the shrubs.

"Almost twenty years, and your parents haven't looked for you. Either they couldn't, didn't care to, or figured you were dead. If they weren't dead themselves," George said.

It never occurred to me that it might be my parents' job to find me. I always thought it was up to me.

"It's happened to all of us, Perry," George continued. "Me, Alice, all the men and women on the wind farm. Every one of us has survived chaos and abandonment, lost family and partners. We're all orphans. But you have to understand, there's a place for you here. And you can stay as long as you want."

I felt the map in my mind shifting. I recalled Otis's stories about how the continents were once all together and then drifted apart and imagined my mind a miniature Earth. Otis's stories about my parents flashed by, and I saw my father roping a deer. I felt myself smile and wondered if George noticed, or whether, as I, he was looking out into the darkness at the shrubs and jackrabbits.

Perhaps it is because I am living in civilization now, and not the abandoned natural world, that I have trouble feeling the presence of the singing wolves. I don't completely understand this world and don't consider myself completely in it. Working in the garden at the wind farm is nothing like working in the garden at White Earth River. Perhaps because the food I grow is extra, better tasting and fresher than the food everyone ate before, but extra. If we shut down the garden tomorrow, we'd still have vegetables for dinner. Alice would take a package out of the freezer or open a can. Not as good as vegetables from the garden, but vegetables nevertheless. We wouldn't starve.

Sometimes I regard George and Alice as my parents. They live together, but they aren't married and don't share a bed, as Nola and I did and as Otis and Malèna once did. George and Alice are friends. They drink tequila and eat meals together. Sometimes they hug each other, but only as friends. Alice is saving herself for Sunny, her lover, who was relocated to the Center. George, I don't know if he was married. He hasn't mentioned a woman, a man, or children, and he looks too old for national reproductive service. George treats me well, as well as Otis did, but I don't spend as much time with him as I did with Otis.

Alice first told me her story about losing her restaurant and Sunny one day while she was cutting up a basket of onions that I had pulled from the garden. "Imagine," she likes to say, "if you had ended up in the Center and bumped into Sunny." I don't think that either possibility was likely, but I don't tell her this because the idea of being in the Center seems to please her. She still thinks that someday she'll be allowed to join Sunny. I would be sorry if she left.

In the evenings while the workers are eating and Alice and George are drinking tequila, I swim in the pool by myself. The pool reminds me of the deep holes in the White Earth River, although the water in the pool looks blue, because of the paint on the bottom and sides, instead of muddy green like the river. When I finish my swim, I sit at the wooden table in my small adobe house.

It's sited in a grove of date palms, not far from the swimming pool. The dates fall on the ground, and I collect them to eat at night. They're sweet. The house has a flat roof and is built of a mud mixture. Timbers line the ceiling, as in the cave, and a wooden bed frame and shelf for a lamp occupy one end of the room, a wooden dresser is situated along a wall, and a wooden chair and table are just inside the door. The table and shelf have the same type of lamps on them, a metal rod to hide the wire and a paper shade that dulls the light bulb to yellow. I rarely use the lamps. On the ceiling is a third light, which I discovered just recently. There's enough space for me to walk back and forth between the bed and the table. Instead of willow mats, a wool rug woven in bright red, white, green, yellow, and black stripes covers part of the floor, which is concrete. A sink and toilet are hidden in a corner behind a screen of three old carved wooden doors hinged together. Eight windows, four sets of two side by side, break up the walls.

Sometimes I imagine my house as being in White Earth River, on the terrace below Windy Butte, instead of the Coachella Valley. If it were, I wouldn't need electricity; my eight windows and door would surround me with more light than two lamps and a ceiling light could ever provide.

I like to keep the door open, the windows, too, with the curtains pulled back so at night I can look at the stars, the outline of the palms against the dark-blue sky. I listen for birds. A white owl lives in one of the palms. Sometimes it hoots.

Since I cannot build a fire in the house, I turn on the electric light and stare at it. This helps me think about the map in my head, how it is now stretched over the continent to include the five people I've known, all of whom have addressed me by a name different from the one my parents gave me, assuming they did name me, which I will never know.

Otis was the only person I loved, truly loved. I think about him every day and worry that I am so far from the juniper that his spirit will never find me. I regret that he died. I regret that we aren't of the same blood and that I won't be able to pass his blood on to my children.

I think a little bit about the stranger, but not too much, about how the currents took him to the bottom of the lake, where, as far as I know, he remains. I didn't see his face, the expression on it, before he slipped below the surface. This bothers me; I don't know why. I remember how it looked, earlier, when he was struggling to stay afloat: the pain, the sense of not knowing what was happening, the fear. Did he look that way when he went under? Or did he close his eyes? Or open his mouth to speak, only to have water fill his throat? I regret that he drowned, that I wasn't able to save him. I didn't want to kill him. I just wanted him to leave me alone.

Other than Otis, I think the most about Nola. I suppose I loved her—for the couple of weeks that we spent together, anyway. I have tried to forgive her for leaving me but so far haven't been able to. And if our lovemaking led to a child, well, that's all the more reason not to do so. Alice said it is unlikely that Nola would've gotten pregnant unless it was the right time of the month. Our last sex, and any semen that Nola may have been able to carry away inside her, was a souvenir, a remembrance, Alice says, nothing more.

Only once has Alice shouted at me and defended Nola. She said that my beliefs about Nola were "naive," that what Nola had done—offer me a chance to flee to the Center—was noble, and she only left me when she realized that I hadn't fallen in love with her and was unwilling to give up my self-delusions. "You should have been grateful," Alice said, "but no, you rejected your chance for a partner, a better life. Meanwhile, think of poor Nola, perhaps alone, maybe with your child."

I don't agree with Alice and think her defense of Nola is shaped by her own desire to be with Sunny in the Center. And maybe, too, the fact that she's a woman and sometimes takes Nola's side in the story. But I haven't remained angry with her. I know she cares about me. She's given me a tablet of paper. "You should write down what happened, so you'll remember," she said.

"How could I forget?" I asked. "I remember everything that's ever happened to me."

"You'd be surprised," she said. "When you get old."

"But can't I take medicine?" I explained how Nola's parents had been extended.

"The government wouldn't offer that to you," she said. "So you need a record, for your children or a partner, if you meet someone and stay with them for a long time."

Alice hasn't kept a record of her life and says she's too old to start now. Sometimes I wonder if she's tired of hearing my story or worries that I'm tired of hearing hers or wants me to include her story along with mine. I suppose a little bit of everyone whom I've met will appear in my record. Nola filmed some of our time together with her hedgehog, and I wonder if she can remember me without pictures and movies. Or perhaps she doesn't bother looking at them anymore. Perhaps she's forgotten the sound of my voice.

For a long time I didn't know what to call my story. I couldn't come up with a fancy title as Otis had done for the story about his fake vision. Alice suggested I call it "During-the-Event," my name, since it's a story about me. I guess that's as good of a title as any.

One thing I have agreed to, which both Alice and George consider "positive," is to attend the dance the wind farm is hosting. Gaz will be there. Gaz is the woman who delivers chickens to the wind farm. She lives on an agriculture preserve in the Owens River Valley, which is a small farming district. The main region is still the Central Valley, but government planners decided that since Angeles del Este is much smaller than old Los Angeles, not as much water needed to be diverted to the coast. The Owens River Valley has some adequate soil, as it turns out, and its vegetables and animals support the solar facility in the desert east of the Owens River and also our wind farm.

Gaz is short for Gazelle, which isn't her original name. Her parents named her Jennifer when she was born, but once she was old enough to run, they began calling her Gazelle because she has long legs and is thin and pranced when she ran, like the African gazelle they had seen in nature films, her parents told her. Eventually, she changed her name legally to Gazelle, just Gazelle, no family name.

Alice introduced us one day when Gaz made a delivery. We haven't spent much time together. She delivers the chickens once a week in late morning. They are already slaughtered, so we can put them in the freezer without further preparation. Once we unload the chickens, it is time for lunch, which Alice lets Gaz and me eat alone together in the kitchen. Gaz grew up on a small sheep farm in the Owens River Valley. Her parents divorced when she was in school.

Her mother moved away, but her father stayed on the farm. Gaz was living in another town in the eastern Sierra, Bishop, when the government started to reduce the population of the continent. Her father was spared because he was a farmer, and he arranged for her to work for him. She doesn't know what happened to her mother. She was living in San Francisco.

I like the fact that she has a name that isn't her original one. We have this in common. Also, she lost one of her parents. I like talking to her. She's quieter than Nola was and not as muscular, though she isn't weak. She can carry a couple chickens in each hand when we unload her truck.

Alice and George think it would be fun if Gaz and I danced together, as a way of getting to know each other better. I told them that the dancing I've done alone to grieve Otis's death wouldn't be proper to do with other people. They said that no one would know about the story behind my movements and that everyone unleashed their own wild steps when the music started. Then they both laughed and told me to get plenty of rest and drink a lot of water beforehand. They assured me that I was going to sweat. So I am awaiting this. The dance is next Saturday.

ACKNOWLEDGMENTS

Many readers critiqued my manuscript over the years, and their comments were invaluable in guiding its revision. I'd like to thank Jan Jaffe; Sybille Pearson, Don Raney, Phyllis Raphael, Louise Rose, and Steve Schrader; Susan Thomas; Greg Hrbek; students at the NY State Summer Writers Institute; Howard Norman; Dan Wigutow and Caroline Moore; Liz Cross; Will Nixon; James Rahn; Louise Fabiani; Alice Peck; Elizabeth Mitchell; and Christopher Rhodes.

Thanks to Andrew Luft and Daryl Farmer and *Permafrost Magazine* for hosting a literary contest; to Nate Bauer, Dana Henricks, Jen Gunderson, Martin Schmoll, Laura Walker, and Krista West, and the University of Alaska Press for putting it all together; and to Wiley Saichek for helping spread the word.

ROGER WALL

Roger Wall lived throughout the United States before ending up at the University of North Carolina at Chapel Hill, where he studied fiction writing. He lives in New York and the Catskills.

During-the-Event is the 2018 Permafrost Book Prize in Fiction.